BEYOND PLATFORM 13

EVA IBBOTSON
SIBÉAL POUNDER

VIKING

VIKING

An imprint of Penguin Random House LLC, New York

First published in the United Kingdom by Macmillan Children's Books,
an imprint of Pan Macmillan, 2019

This edition first published in the United States of America by Viking,
an imprint of Penguin Random House LLC, 2021

Visit us online at penguinrandomhouse.com.

Library of Congress Cataloging-in-Publication Data is available.

Printed in the United States of America

ISBN 9780593204177

1 3 5 7 9 10 8 6 4 2

Design by Opal Roengchai
Text set in P22 Stickley Pro

PROLOGUE

NO ONE noticed the young woman in bright blue boots walking along the platform at Vienna Central Station. I suppose you could argue she was easy to miss: just an average-height teenager with a long black bob and mismatched eyes of green and brown. She had always hated how human she looked, but even she had to admit it came in useful sometimes.

A man with a face as angry as crumpled paper was the only one to spot her. She was in his way, so he barged straight into her, as if the platform belonged more to him than it did to her.

"WATCH WHERE YOU'RE GOING, LADY!" he shouted as they collided.

Odge Gribble didn't break her stride as she turned and said, "It's *hag*, actually."

CHAPTER ONE

LINA LASKY

LINA LASKY believed in almost every kind of magic. She believed in wizard spells and witches' potions and sometimes even in the people who pull rabbits out of hats, depending on the party. She saw mermaids in her dreams and trolls dancing with vegetables. Once, when daydreaming, she'd imagined the fluffiest of mystical creatures, plump like a little pillow, with a whiskery nose and huge black eyes—a little bit like a seal, only without the flippers. She'd immediately refashioned her pom-pom backpack to look just like her vision.

All her friends had stopped believing in magic long ago, but that's the thing about magic—it's only real if you believe in it. Though Lina didn't know it, the things she imagined were very real—even the trolls dancing with vegetables.

"If magical creatures are real, then they must be hiding somewhere," Lina said to her mother and father one day over breakfast. There's no better time to discuss magic than over some good cereal or toast. "A hairy hag or a fairy wouldn't be able to blend in, so they must all *be somewhere else*. A place we haven't found yet."

Of course, her parents barely listened; adults rarely do when you speak of magic. The more wrinkles a person has, the less tolerance they have for things like that. They want proof.

"We have a surprise," her father said, trying to change the subject.

"We're taking you to see your aunt in Salzburg for your birthday! A whole long weekend, all of us together!" Lina's mother grinned as she handed over the train tickets. "Surprise! Oh, and I'm almost *positive* that your aunt's neighbor is a *hag*," she added, hoping to sweeten the deal.

"That's a terrible thing to say about Mrs. Frampton," her father scoffed.

"It's a huge compliment, actually," Lina corrected him. "I would do anything to meet a hag! They can grow hair out of their ears and tell the weather with their eyelashes—or, at least, that's what the stories say. I'd say Mrs. Frampton's more of a witch, though."

"Oh really, Lina!" Her mother laughed. "Your imagination is something else."

Lina paused, her fork hovering over her plate. She did occasionally worry she might be wrong.

"Right—come on, Lina," her father said. "Grab your seal backpack."

"It's a magical being," Lina said, hugging her backpack defensively.

"Of course, *magical being*," her mother said with a small smile.

Her father took her plate away and pulled out her chair. "Come on, you magical being, or we'll miss our train."

Lina grabbed her backpack from the car boot and slung it over her shoulder. She'd teamed it with a chunky jumper, jeans, and her favorite silver trainers. She didn't like the station at that time in the morning.

"It smells of coffee and damp hair."

"Your mother has taken time off work especially for your birthday, Lina," her father whispered. "Try to be a little more enthusiastic."

Lina dragged her feet along the platform, and then she saw her, just up ahead—a teenager in bright blue boots. Lina watched as a man rudely barged into her. But then the most peculiar thing happened: he bounced off her as though she were nothing but bones and magic. The teenager turned and mouthed something at the man. Something that looked a lot like—

"HAG!" Lina shouted.

And then everything went black.

CHAPTER TWO

MAGDELENA

THERE WAS a finger click, and the lights came back on.

"Where's everyone gone?" Lina cried, staring down the empty platform.

The hag looked confused. "What do you mean, where's everyone gone?"

"The people," Lina spluttered. "My parents!"

"You brought your parents on a secret royal mission?" the hag asked with a raised eyebrow. "Well, I suppose you are young. Much younger than I thought you'd be, actually . . ."

"Are they gone *forever*?" Lina asked, suddenly feeling very worried.

The hag looked up Lina's nose. "Are you unwell? Have you got the Dribbly Ribblets? The Spotted-Tongue Munchflu? Terror Tibtoms?"

Lina stared at her, completely bewildered, before eventually replying, "I *hope* not."

"I used Lost Laces," the hag explained, holding up some shimmering silver laces. "All I had to do was give them a little pull, and we became invisible to everyone, and everyone became invisible to us. They're all still here—we just can't see them, and they can't see us."

Lina watched as a coffee cup sailed past her head.

"The less the humans see, the better. It's safer if we keep this meeting a secret, I'm sure you'll agree. The laces don't last long. Bit of a gimmick, really. That old witch who likes to sunbathe with the mutant mermaids on our island invented them. I think her mermaid friends were annoyed that she spent so long inventing a magic product they could never use."

"Oh," Lina said, "because mermaids don't have feet and have no need for shoes or laces. I get it."

The hag scrunched up her face. "No. Mutant mermaids *do* have feet—that's what makes them mutant. They were annoyed because they have fins for hands, so they can't *tie* shoelaces. Anyway, don't worry about the temporary vanishing nature of the Lost Laces. Hans, my ogre friend, is bringing the stronger stuff for the big journey later, so you will be completely hidden." She eyed Lina's backpack. "Ben is going to be so pleased to meet you. When I sent you the letter, things were bad—but now they're even worse."

Lina stared at the hag. "Ben? Letter?" But the hag wasn't listening.

"Time to go. Magdelena is collecting us. I told her we could walk, but she insisted. I'm sure her reputation precedes her here in Vienna."

Lina nodded slowly, though she had no idea who the hag was talking about. "Yes—I've heard Magdelena is a very . . . funny woman."

"Funny!" The hag laughed. "Ha, you're a scream! She's bossy and sometimes terrifying, and she's certainly not a woman. Now HOLD ON, PLEASE. It's going to get ROCKY." She offered Lina her arm.

Lina grabbed hold of it, bewildered and half expecting the ground to explode and some sort of wondrous troll woman to burst from the floor. But it wasn't that at all.

A tiny ghostly carriage no bigger than a cat and pulled by two aged ghost pigeons squeaked along the platform slowly, before eventually grinding to a halt in front of them.

"I'm just messing with you!" the hag said, patting Lina's back. "You don't need to hold on. Magdelena's tiny."

A ghost rat wearing a chunky pearl necklace poked her head out the carriage door. "Hello, Odge! Still no ear hair or warts, I see."

The hag shrugged. "I live in hope!" She took the ghost rat's paw in her hand and stroked it with her thumb. Her bright blue nail polish matched her boots perfectly. "It's good to see you, Magdelena. It's been too long."

Lina stumbled backward in disbelief and tripped over a suitcase.

"Oh, that's my case," Odge said, grabbing it and throwing it into the carriage. It shrank down to just the right size and slotted neatly inside.

Stunned, Lina grabbed a floating cup of coffee and downed it. She knew adults drank coffee to wake up, so maybe it would shake her out of this strange dream. It just made her feel a bit sick.

Odge leaned down and stared into the carriage. "Plenty of room for us!"

"It's rat-sized!" Lina cried. "There's no room for us at all!"

Magdelena looked down her nose at Lina. "Are you sure she's the right one?"

Odge swiveled Lina round and showed Magdelena her backpack. "Positive! That's a fluffy mistmaker, all right!"

"A what?" Lina whispered.

"Subtle," Magdelena said sarcastically. "The humans won't suspect a thing."

"Word on the Island is she's an elusive character—likes to hide away. We weren't sure she would even come," Odge mumbled to Magdelena. "Bold fashion choices, though! Although I had heard she likes elaborate hats, not backpacks. Rumors are so rarely correct."

"Well, it's now or never. The laces are wearing off," Magdelena said, nodding at a man's mustache appearing behind them. "If you want to travel to the Island, we need to get out of here now."

Lina's eyes lit up. "Island? Is that where you all hide? You're a hag from a secret island!"

"She's only the most famous hag," Magdelena scoffed. "She saved our prince, dear girl!"

Lina gawped at Odge.

Odge scuffled her blue boots awkwardly; clearly she wasn't fond of the attention.

"Everyone knows Odge Gribble!" Magdelena went on. "She's a very big deal. You're lucky to meet her. *Everyone* wants to meet Odge."

"You did get my letter, didn't you?" Odge asked, standing in front of Magdelena to stop her talking. "I did sign it *Odge Gribble*, and I did say I would meet you right here."

It was in that moment, as her parents started to fizzle back into view, that Lina Lasky had a decision to make.

"WHEEEEEEEEEE!" Lina cried, as they tore through the streets of Vienna in a ghostly carriage steered by a gossiping dead rat.

"And Mariella Crockit blocked all the toilets in the hotel this morning by trying to smuggle in her mermaid friend. I said, *Mariella Crockit, I'd possibly accept a freshwater mermaid at my hotel, but not a sewer one!* I think in the last nine years they've forgotten just what kind of establishment my hotel is!"

Odge chewed on her bottom lip and nodded absently. Lina could tell she didn't approve of Magdelena's snobbery.

"And you would not *believe* what Netty Pruddle's mother got up to yesterday afternoon."

Lina watched as Odge snapped to attention.

"Netty Pruddle's mother?"

Magdelena let out a long sigh. "Yes. She only

went and trotted downstairs to the spa! I said, *Mrs. Pruddle, as one of the wartiest hags we have ever known in our community, I would kindly ask you to refrain from getting back massages from humans. It'll raise suspicions!* To be perfectly honest, Odge, this year, with everything going on on the Island, it has been quite trying."

"I thought Mrs. Pruddle was helping to get everyone organized to battle the harpies?" Odge said, leaning forward as the carriage rattled past huge human shoes stomping the pavements. Each footstep echoed in Lina's ears and made the carriage bounce.

"Mrs. Pruddle has had to scale back her involvement since her daughter was selected to compete to be a handmaid to the new harpy . . ." She paused and gagged. "*Queen.* They worried it might affect Netty's chance of winning if her mother had disappeared with the rebellion, so instead she's pretending to be on a spa holiday here. I wish she had chosen another hotel."

Odge punched the air, sending her fist through the roof of the carriage. Once any part of you exited the ghost carriage, you were once again back to normal size. So anyone walking along the Philharmoniker Strasse at that very moment would've seen a fist attached to nobody at all, sailing triumphantly through the air. Luckily no one did, or this story would have been over before it had barely begun.

"Netty's my hag friend," Odge said excitedly to Lina. "And she did it! She got into the competition! She's on our side. She's going to infiltrate the harpy lair by pretending to be a maid. She's our very big eyes on the inside!"

Lina was about to respond when Magdelena put her foot on the brakes and catapulted them from the carriage into the Sacher Hotel's foyer. Lina looked up to see the hotel porter looming over them. She quickly untangled herself from Odge and jumped to her feet.

"Act natural," Odge whispered to Lina. So Lina pretended she was inspecting the ceiling.

"Ah," the porter said with a disapproving glance. "Welcome back, Miss Gribble."

Lina watched Magdelena and her carriage disappear down the corridor and through a wall. The porter clearly hadn't noticed the ghost rat; Lina thought he looked like the kind of person who would scream in such situations.

All around them, people dressed in their finest clothes glided past. Lina stood tall, trying to look as grown up as possible.

"Finished sightseeing so soon?" he said. "Shall

I carry your bags to your room?" He eyed Odge's suitcase first and then Lina's fluffy backpack, stifling a smirk. It didn't exactly fit with the grand hotel, but then she had made it herself, which was more than she could say for all the other people with bags in there.

Odge glanced at the clock above the lifts and frowned. "We're too early, but we don't want to loiter upstairs—it's too risky."

"I beg your pardon?" the man said.

Odge stiffened as she seemed to realize she'd been thinking aloud. "We'll be taking cake in the café before we go upstairs."

They sidestepped awkwardly past the man.

"We can't hang around the gump," Odge explained as they took the corridor to the hotel café, passing well-watered plants and well-watered people.

"Gump?" Lina mumbled.

"Yes, the gump!" Odge said. "I think everyone assumes the only gump in Vienna is in the mountains, but there is also the special one, right here in the hotel. It was mostly used by important people from our magical island—royals, trolls with award-winning hair, people like that. Vienna is the only country in the world with two gumps; everywhere else just has one."

"And you use the gumps to get to your island?" Lina asked excitedly.

Odge stopped dead in her tracks. "Of course! What else would you use a gump for? And, yes, although calling it *the Island* is quite formal. Us young ones just call it *Mist*."

Lina wiggled with excitement. "So a gump is a portal to another world—a magical world called Mist."

"Well, obviously," Odge said. "Now, shall we have some milk and chocolate cake before we save the world?"

Lina gulped. "Pardon?"

Odge grinned. "I saved a prince, and—now I've found you—you are going to save our island." She spotted Lina's panicked expression. "Oh, don't worry! *After* cake."

CHAPTER THREE

THE MISTMAKER

LINA WAS trying to work out just who Odge thought she was as they took a seat in the sumptuous café and were brought tall glasses of milk.

They sat in silence, staring at each other.

"Nice boots," Lina eventually said.

Odge opened her mouth wide. "Mank moo, mey match my meeth."

At the very back of Odge's mouth, Lina could see she had a bright blue molar.

"Your back tooth is blue!" Lina cried. "Is that a hag thing? You don't look much like a hag."

"And you don't look much like the world's oldest and only mistmaker expert."

"Mistmaker expert?" Lina took her chance. "Well, actually . . . about that—I think you've got the wrong—"

But Odge interrupted her. "For a long time, I wished I had boils and warts scattered across my face in fun patterns, and long ear hairs that I could braid, like my older sisters. It was all I wanted. But then I grew up and realized I might not be hag perfection, but who cares. I took all the time I used to spend wishing I could look different, and instead I started doing fun things, like rock-monster climbing, dancing with my friend Gurkie, and eating delicious snacks. I've got a list of ones to try and everything." She took out a notebook and scratched *Torte in Vienna* off the list.

ODGE'S DELICIOUS SNACK LIST OF HAG PERFECTION

HANS-OME CHEESES CHOC-CHEESE CHUNK
GURKIE'S CARROT CAKE
COR'S ENCHANTED TRIFLE
FISH AND CHIPS WITH ERNIE
TEA AND TOAST IN LONDON
~~TORTE IN VIENNA~~

The waiter arrived with the chocolate cake and placed it down on the table delicately and with all the precision of a world-class surgeon. Odge fell forward and smooshed her face into it.

Lina tried not to laugh as the waiter choked back a gasp and walked off, his face almost identical to someone who had just been dunked in a sewer.

"This is how we eat on the Island of Mist," Odge whispered to Lina as she came up for air.

Lina wasn't sure whether to believe Odge or not.

"No, I'm messing with you!" Odge said with a snort. "I just wanted to put my face in a cake. I highly recommend it, every once in a while. It's relaxing."

"But not in *public*," Lina said, noticing people were staring.

"The more public, the better," Odge said with a cakey wink. "I mean, has your face really been smooshed in a cake if no one is there to see it?"

Lina bit into the Sachertorte—a delicious soft chocolate sponge with apricot jam—and cast her eye around the room. A grand piano sat unattended in the corner as diners tucked into cakes and laughed merrily. She wondered if her parents were worried, and if she'd made a terrible mistake. It seemed the hag thought she was some sort of superhero who was going to save her island. Or maybe that had been another one of Odge's jokes. Yes—perhaps that wasn't what she meant at all. She stuffed more cake in her mouth, stuffing the worry down with it.

"I forgot to ask your name!" Odge cried. "Or do you prefer *the mistmaker master*? I could understand that; it is more formal."

"Lina is fine," Lina said, gulping down the cake.

"Well, you can call me Odge. That's what everyone calls me, apart from Ben. He tends to call me Gribs."

They sat in awkward silence once more.

"So, do you like living in the human world, Lina?" Odge asked.

"I like Vienna," Lina said, which was true. "It's full of beauty and music. They say everyone in Vienna gets dunked in opera." She took a big swig of her milk.

"I have an aunt who lives in London," Odge said, playing with her napkin. "She's the only one in our family who lives in the human world. She's my favorite relative, and she's excellent at balding people."

Odge's suitcase shuffled forward.

"What's in your suitcase?" Lina asked nervously, gripping the arms of her chair.

"It's Ray," Odge whispered, leaning so far forward her bobbed hair dipped into the milk. She glanced around her and then, when assured the coast was clear, slowly unbuckled the case. "Ben and I named him after someone we knew many years ago. He's Ben's pet, really, but I like to think we share him."

She pulled out a fluffy white bundle with saucer-sized eyes. It was shaking nervously.

Lina stared at the little thing in disbelief. It looked just like her magical-being backpack, only smaller and a lot more alive.

"Can I hold him?" Lina asked excitedly.

Odge winked and sneakily passed him under the table. Lina could feel his soft fur between her fingers. He felt silky and tense like a rabbit, but his belly was rounded and solid like a bird's.

"Now, the plan," Odge said.

Lina pulled the tablecloth farther over the creature to keep him cozy. He seemed perfectly happy on her lap, peeking out at the other diners.

"Hans is bringing the fernseed so we can travel through the gump undetected," Odge explained. "I'm sure I don't need to tell you that, with everything going on, our bringing you to the Island must remain a secret."

Lina gulped down some torte, feeling it slide uneasily into her knotted stomach. "Um, what exactly is it you need me to do?"

"Use your expertise, of course," Odge said, patting the suitcase.

"And my expertise is . . . making bags?" Lina guessed.

Milk shot from Odge's nose as she rolled back on her chair in a fit of giggles. "Oh, you're so funny! And *modest*."

Just then, a woman in a ball gown glided into the room and took a seat at the piano to much applause.

"Oh no," Odge said, whipping the creature from Lina's grasp and trying to coax him into the case. He didn't seem to want to go back in.

The woman in the ball gown began plucking the keys of the piano before launching into a song that Lina recognized as Mozart's Piano Concerto No. 21. It was one of her favorites.

Odge buckled up the case quickly, but it was too late—mist began to seep from the seams, coating Odge's hands until they, and most of the table, were under a cloud.

"The music has set him off," Odge said in a panic. "And he hasn't been producing mist on the Island no matter how much music we play. There's more mist than usual—he must have a backlog!"

"Well, we should go," Lina whispered urgently.

Odge nodded, grabbing what was left of both

slices of chocolate torte and stuffing them in her pockets.

"Is that smoke?" a woman cried from a nearby table. "Smoking is not allowed in here."

"Oh dear—I lit my pipe without thinking," Odge said in a deep voice.

"She doesn't have a pipe!" a man cried. "She has a smoking suitcase!"

People started to scream.

Odge made for the door. Lina followed, stumbling around tables and knocking over teacups just to keep up with her. The mist grew thicker. The music grew louder.

"Oh no," Lina heard Odge groan, just as a gigantic furry thing burst from the case and bobbed along to the song in the foyer.

"Didn't I tell you in my letter weird things were happening to the mistmakers?" Odge said, gesturing at an oversized Ray. "I've never seen this before. He's absolutely *massive*!"

"So it's called a *mistmaker*," Lina breathed, staring at it in awe.

"BEAR!" someone roared.

"FUR MONSTER!" yelled another.

"Don't panic," Odge said, trying to push Ray toward the lifts. "We need to get him upstairs, undetected."

Bit late for that, Lina thought as the mistmaker continued to grow until he was more than twice her height.

They reached the lifts just as Magdelena appeared with a pop.

"Odge Gribble! As our hero hag, this is not the kind of incompetent display of obvious magic I expect from you!" Magdelena turned her attention to Lina. "Well, can't you do something? You *are* the mistmaker expert, after all."

Lina stared blankly at the little ghost rat, trying to ignore the sounds of screams and smashing plates down the corridor. "Me? Oh no, you see, I've been trying to tell Odge—"

"Yes . . . *quickly*—what do you advise?" Magdelena asked, her voice a mix of fear and frustration.

"Err . . . get the pianist to stop playing?" Lina guessed. "It was the music that set him off. He'll almost certainly shrink back if it stops."

Magdelena scuttled off toward the piano, claws out, while Lina and Odge tried to push the mistmaker into the lift.

"We just need to get to the fourth floor," Odge said, panting.

There was a high-pitched squeal from the pianist, and the music suddenly cut out.

Lina coughed as the mist began to clear. They looked up hopefully at Ray, but he wasn't showing any signs of shrinking.

"WHAT IS THAT THING?" a man cried, dropping his shopping.

"It's . . . MY FURRY UNCLE!" Odge yelled unconvincingly. "HE'S SO HAPPY TO BE HERE THAT HE'S COMBUSTING WITH EXCITEMENT!" She turned to Lina. "Can human uncles do that? That's believable, isn't it?"

"Now what?" Magdelena snapped as she reappeared at their feet and put her claws away. "The pianist is cowering in the corner. There's chocolate torte smeared on the walls . . ."

Lina saw Odge lick her lips at the thought.

"The humans are getting more than a bit suspicious!" Magdelena finished.

Odge and Lina quickly pushed Ray into the lift and squeezed in behind him. Odge hit the button for floor four.

"They'll just think it was a performance piece or something," Odge said to Lina. "Or my furry uncle. I'd believe that if I were a human. He's furry, and I think he has the face of an uncle."

Magdelena clutched her pearls as the lift doors closed. "You, Odge Gribble, are worse than Mariella Crockit and Mrs. Pruddle *combined*!"

The fourth floor was where the gump was hidden, in the Hansel and Gretel suite. The magical creatures had done their utmost to keep the humans from exiting the lift on that floor. Hundreds of STOP! CLEANING IN PROGRESS signs peppered the hallway, and mops lay crisscrossed all over the floor like a broom-cupboard forest.

Ray bounded right through them, snapping at their handles as he went.

Magdelena jumped onto Lina's shoulder. "Every nine years when the gump opens, the hags hire out the whole fourth floor. I task myself with keeping them in order."

A naked hag covered in rainbow-colored boils catapulted herself down the hallway and into the lift.

"STOP TRYING TO USE THE SPA, MRS. PRUDDLE!" Magdelena roared as she leaped from Lina's shoulder and scuttled fast toward the rebellious hag.

Lina kept on down the corridor, trying to keep up with Odge. She pushed mops out of the way and stepped over buckets. They stopped at the Hansel and Gretel suite.

"Hans should be here any minute," Odge said,

standing tall, though Lina could detect a drop of worry in her voice.

They didn't have to wait long; it was only moments before the door to the Hansel and Gretel suite flew open and a long line of trolls marched out, many of them crying.

Odge bowed her head respectfully, and Lina did the same.

"Why are they crying?" Lina asked.

"Wouldn't you, if you were told to leave your home forever? The harpies seized power the night the gump opened, knowing that it only opens every nine years for nine days. That gave them nine days to rid the Island of all the creatures they decided didn't belong there anymore." Odge sighed. "It's all truly awful. And, of course, harpies hate humans most of all, so we'll have to sneak you in."

Lina nodded. "Actually—about that. I wanted to tell you something—"

"Oh, I think I see Hans!" Odge said, standing on her tiptoes to get a better view inside the suite.

Magical creatures continued to spill out the door: wizards riding floating trunks, witches with armfuls of potion bottles and hats, a two-headed mermaid in a cauldron, and creatures

Lina didn't even know the names of—but Odge informed her were banshees, nuckelavees, and sky yelpers—and five gorgeously sweet-smelling flower fairies.

"IS ME!" came a booming voice.

"AND THERE HE IS!" Odge cheered.

Lina looked up to see an ogre with a mustard-yellow beard and toothy grin bounding toward them, a gigantic ray of sunshine in an otherwise gloomy lineup. He smelled a lot like cheese. He thrust his scrunched-up fist in Odge's face, unfurling his fingers to reveal a small bottle.

"Hans!" Odge said, jumping up high to hug the giant round his shoulders. "You're my hero."

"Is nothing—nothing at all," Hans said, blushing.

"This is the mistmaker expert," Odge said. "Her name is Lina."

Hans beamed at Lina before shifting his gaze to the mistmaker.

He gasped. "RAY IS SO BIG! WHAT 'APPEN TO 'IM?"

"Mozart," Odge explained. "He's fine . . . If my theory is correct, I suspect he'll shrink back when we return to Mist."

Hans pointed slowly at Odge, then Ray, then

Lina, then himself, as if counting. He knitted his eyebrows together and said, "No."

Odge looked up. "No what, Hans?"

"The fernseed. I stay."

Odge stared at the bottle. "Oh no, this is a problem. Ray is so big that we don't have enough to cover him *and* you and Hans. Hags are allowed on the Island still, so I can walk straight in, but no humans or ogres. And they hate mistmakers, which I just can't believe, given the mistmakers are the ones who make the mist to keep our island protected. They don't think they need them! I can't mess this up—we need to figure out a solution to this fernseed problem."

"I'll stay," Lina said, realizing she was in over her head. "And I'll stay because I'm not—"

"You're the most important one, Lina!" Odge interrupted. "You are a must. But then so is Ray. He can't look after himself, so we can't leave him. Plus all the humans downstairs think he's a furry uncle, and I just don't think he'll be able to keep that facade up on his own."

"Please," Hans said with a sweet smile. "I see parents in Vienna; tell them about the cheeses."

"Hans owns an incredibly successful cheese shop in the Mist mountains called Hans-ome Cheeses," Odge explained to Lina. "As the mistmaker expert, you'll get first pick of the smelliest ones."

"But I'm not—" Lina tried again, but Hans wailed before she could finish.

"IS GONE! Harpies got to the mountain."

Lina could see Odge's eye twitch. "Yes, I'm sorry—I almost forgot. Well, Hans . . . it *was* the best cheese shop on Mist, and it will be again before the gump closes. I'll get it back from the harpies—I promise you I will."

Hans put his hands on his hips proudly as Lina smiled at him. She liked Hans a lot, and the thought of leaving him behind was making her sad—and she'd only known him for two minutes.

"Hans," Odge managed to squeak, tears running down her cheeks, "I will fix everything, and then you can come home."

"Why can't Hans just walk back through the gump?" Lina asked. "Why do we have to be hidden?"

Odge sighed. "Ogres are being evicted, along with everyone else. Now Hans has exited the Island, there is no going back. Not until we save Mist and stop the harpies. And they'll never let Ray in looking like *that*. The plan was that Hans would walk through the gump, pretending to be leaving the Island of Mist forever, but then he'd meet us here, we'd cover him and you in fernseed and sneak you back through. But now there's not enough because Ray is inconveniently the size of Hans!"

Ray blinked at them with his unfathomably huge saucer eyes.

"There's only one thing for it," Odge said, uncorking the bottle and smearing fernseed hastily on Lina's feet before she could stop her. It was gloopy, like thick mustard, and peppered with prickly seeds that scratched her skin. A warm feeling crept slowly up her legs. It felt like being dipped in sun-drenched sand.

Odge leaned so close to Lina their noses were practically touching. "How do you feel?"

"Heavy," Lina said as she looked down and saw her legs disappear. Her stomach felt heavy too, weighed down by what was happening— Odge had wasted the fernseed on her, an ordinary human girl, not a mistmaker expert.

"And now you're hidden," Odge said, smearing the remaining paste over Ray's paws.

Lina watched in amazement as the magic worked its way up his body quickly, erasing him until only the very fluffy tip of his head was visible.

They all waited for it to vanish, but it didn't.

"Oh no," Hans said, covering his mouth with his hands. "I see 'im."

Odge pinched the bridge of her nose. "And we're completely out of fernseed?"

Hans nodded vigorously.

Odge groaned just as a harpy flew past. Lina had never seen anything like it—a hideous beast that looked to be a tall, spindly falcon with the face of a furious human. She wore a horrible hat that looked like a pigeon had exploded up there and smelled of rotten intestines. She clasped her handbag tightly in her talons and hissed "yuck" as she passed Hans.

"Don't *yuck* my friend!" Lina shouted angrily. The words charged out before she had time to stop them, and she instantly regretted it.

The harpy screeched to a halt and snapped her head round. "Who said that?"

Lina froze in fear, forgetting for a second that she was invisible.

"Said what?" Odge replied with a gulp. "I love your hat, by the way. It's so . . . dead."

The harpy didn't take her eyes off them as she let herself into the Hansel and Gretel suite.

"Wait," Odge said to the harpy. "You look

familiar—aren't you Miss Jones, one of the important harpies? What are you doing in Vienna?"

"You're mistaken," the harpy snapped, slamming the door behind her.

"Never talk to the harpies, Lina," Odge warned once she had gone. "Even when you're invisible. They have always been sinister creatures, but now that they have power, they don't need to hide it or ever consider they might be wrong. Our world is a dark place on the surface now, not just in hidden corners."

Lina gulped.

"Now," Odge said brightly, "we need to figure out a way to hide the fluffy tip of Ray's head, or we're never going to get home. And we *have* to get back."

Lina wanted desperately to help. "I have an idea," she said. "How bendy is Ray?"

CHAPTER FOUR
THE GUMP

INSIDE THE Hansel and Gretel suite was a room unlike anything Lina could have imagined. She had expected a normal hotel room—a bed, a dresser, a little bathroom—but it was nothing like that at all. For starters, it was narrow and impossibly long. Longer than the whole hotel. Benches lined the sides, many of them empty, and pillows spilled from the coat cupboard. The bathroom, presumably once a place for brushing your teeth and washing your hair, was a swirling vortex filled with stars, its entrance guarded by a sweating harpy with a handbag.

"The gump," Lina whispered, mesmerized by the beauty of it.

"Take a pillow!" the harpy snapped at Odge.

She obliged, plucking a plump pillow from the cupboard. Lina noticed each pillow had a number scrawled on it in what looked like lumpy tooth-paste. She followed behind as Odge made her way to a seat, very carefully, while an almost-invisible Ray crouched close behind her, making it look like the fluffy part of his head was Odge's hat.

"You can't go through before your number is called," Odge muttered out of the corner of her mouth to an invisible Lina. "New evil har-py rules. It shouldn't be too long a wait, given there's hardly anyone here—only a few types of magical creature are allowed through the gump now. The harpies believe the Island is theirs and they should control who lives there. They claim that hundreds of years ago harpies were there first. Seems a strange argument to me. Imag-ine someone racing into this room from the past and saying, 'I sat in that chair you're sitting in first, hundreds of years ago, and so you have to move.' And I'd say, 'But I'm here, sitting in this chair now, and it doesn't belong to you or me, plus you're hundreds of years old, and so this all seems kind of irrelevant.'"

"You make a good point," Lina said.

They sat in silence for a moment, watching the harpy with the pigeon-feather hat pick some-thing out of her teeth with a talon.

"Normally this waiting room would be full," Odge said sadly.

The harpy fixed her eyes on the blank space where Lina sat. Lina held her breath, unsure whether or not the harpy could see her. Perhaps she had overheard them.

"Isn't it marvelous to see such an empty room with only the *right* kind of creatures in it?" the harpy said.

Odge swallowed hard, seemingly pushing down what she really wanted to say. "Yes, glorious," she managed.

"NUMBER NINE, WE'RE ALL FINE. THAT'S NUMBER NINE," chimed the sweaty harpy guarding the gump.

The harpy sitting across from them checked the pillow she was holding. A large number nine was scrawled on it in minty toothpaste. She flew off, her head held high.

"Bleugh," Odge said as soon as she was gone. She scraped her tongue with her finger as if to remove the word she'd just uttered. "It is *not* glorious."

Lina watched as the little harpy stepped onto the edge of the gump and straightened up her hat. The stars inside the vortex grew blindingly bright before the gump whipped her off her feet and pulled her inside, folding in on itself momentarily as if it were digesting her.

"NUMBER TEN, mmmwellenwhen. NUMBER TEN," the harpy called.

"She can't rhyme anything with ten," Odge said, rolling her eyes. "Come on."

Lina reluctantly followed as Odge wobble-walked toward the gump, struggling to keep Ray in line with her head. Lina wondered how it would feel to fall through the gump. Would it be like tumbling down a hill or being shot into space? She obsessed over the details, watching the stars inside it swirl, and wondering if one could potentially poke her eye out.

The harpy guard eyed Odge's "hat" suspiciously. "WAIT!" she cried, spraying Lina with spit. "That on your head—I know what that is."

Lina's legs turned to jelly. If the harpy discovered Ray, it was all over.

"I can explain—" Odge began, but the harpy held up a spindly talon to silence her.

"You can't get past me with *that*. It's a *floating hat*, and I do believe floating hats are banned."

Odge shot Lina a worried glance as the harpy consulted her rulebook. "Hats . . . hats . . . hats . . . Ah, here we go—"

"It's not a floating hat," Odge protested. "Your

eyes must be wonky. You've been working too hard."

The harpy kicked Odge, sending her tumbling. The fluffy tufts of Ray's head stayed firmly in the air.

"*See*—it's floating," the harpy said, running her talon down the rulebook. She snapped it shut as disappointment flashed across her face. "Ugh, you can go through. It's *talking* hats that are banned. Floating ones are fine."

Odge turned to Lina as she stepped onto the swirling edge of the gump. "Mist is calling," she said with a wink.

Different gumps deliver you to the Island of Mist in different ways. Every magical being and human in on the secret knows that the gump on Platform Thirteen at London's King's Cross Station is the one to take if you prefer a gentle sail to the Island. The one on Tokyo's Shibuya Street crossing is the best option for those who like to arrive by cloud. And the gumps in Vienna are perfect for those who enjoy tunneling underground.

Despite its frantic swirling appearance, Lina was surprised to find the fall through the gump was gentle. (The speed had been altered many years ago after the Witches Society of Teeth Fixers—fondly known as the Maggot Teeth Twelve—protested against the speed of the gump, claiming that at least four thousand witch teeth a year were lost as a result of its reckless swirling. You'd think teeth fixers would be delighted with that—more teeth to fix—but the problem is that witches' teeth are unique and almost impossible to replicate. So the Teeth Fixers had to replace them with human teeth bought at an extortionate price from the Corporation of Tooth Fairies. Understandably, the tooth fairies protested against the protest against the gump speed change, but they were smaller and harder to hear, so they lost.)

How long does it take? Lina wondered as she fell gently down next to Odge and Ray, passing stars and streams of mist as she went.

She wished it would last forever. The air around them began to thicken, and then came the smells of salty seas. A deafening roar of thundering waves grew louder and louder until they landed with a squelch on a mattress of strange jelly creatures.

"That's how long it takes," Odge said, peeling

herself off the slimy lump before helping Lina to her feet too.

Lina prodded one of the slimy creatures with her finger, making it wriggle away. They reminded her of edible jellies—all you would have to do was remove the eyes and replace them with a crown of whipped cream, and the resemblance would be uncanny.

"What *is it*?" Lina whispered.

"Oh, are you from the north of the Island?" Odge asked. "That's a brollachan—they're everywhere in the south. Such gentle creatures, and excellent for breaking falls or hiding secret entrances."

"A brollachan," Lina repeated quietly.

It was dark where they'd landed, save for a few small lanterns hanging on the wall, and all Lina could make out were the rocky walls of a narrow tunnel. A little arrow scratched into nearby rocks read:

CENTER MIST

40 ~~ogre~~ steps; 100 witch, ~~wizard~~, and hag steps; 400,000 harpy and ~~fairy~~ steps; 90 ~~mermaid~~ flops

Lina could see the words *ogre*, *wizard*, *mermaid*, and *fairy* had all been scored out, as if someone didn't want those sorts finding their way there at all. It wouldn't be the most pleasant welcome, she imagined, if you were one of those creatures.

Up ahead, Lina could just make out the harpy from the waiting room earlier. She was walking slowly, her back hunched.

"No flying is allowed in the tunnels," Odge explained when she spotted what Lina was looking at. "Health and safety."

The harpy clawed onward, hitting the wall angrily as she did.

"They're terribly lazy and hate to walk," Odge said. "Not many harpies take the Vienna gump. Actually, not many harpies take *any* gump—they like to stay put on Mist and pretend it's the only place in the world."

A strange sensation spread up Lina's legs, as though she were being dipped in sticky rice.

"Ah," Odge said. "You're coming back. The magic of the Island wipes away fernseed fairly quickly. But never mind—we're almost there."

Lina wasn't so sure—the tunnel weaved on for what looked like miles, and the harpy wasn't nearly at the end yet. She felt a tug on her backpack and fell sideways, straight through a wall of slimy brollachans.

When she opened her eyes, she saw nothing but Odge's boots.

"Welcome," the hag said, hoisting her up and revealing the crowds of magical creatures, "to the most hidden part of our island, and your home for the next few days. Welcome, dear Lina, to the Undermist!"

CHAPTER FIVE

BEN

THE MAKESHIFT city of Undermist was more magical than anything Lina could've imagined. Beyond the hidden brollachan entrance lay houses carved into rocky walls, filled with banished magical creatures spilling from every window. Winding streets trickled on for miles and were lined with brollachans wearing pretty rock decorations on their heads as if they were perfectly pruned shrubs. Fairies walked in deliberately elaborate patterns across the walls, creating glitter art to brighten any dark corners not already illuminated by the witches, who had set their hair on fire to light the way.

Lina had finally found it—the place in the world where the magical creatures were hidden!

"Most of the magical beings you see here normally live aboveground in Center Mist," Odge said. "The harpies seized power right before the gump opened. They'd been planning it for years. On the night the gump opened, they attacked, and some of us managed to hide down here. The harpies don't know about this place. It sits right under the old palace, which they destroyed. The whole town up aboveground is nothing but rubble."

"How long have you been down here?" Lina asked.

"Seven days," Odge said. "But the gump will only stay open for two more, and then, as you know, it will close and won't open again for nine whole years. We need to stop the harpies and get all our banished friends back through the gump before then. We have to bring them home before it's too late. But that's why you're here."

Lina stopped and threw her hands in the air. "ODGE, I *REALLY* NEED TO TELL YOU SOMETHING."

At the sight of the small girl with the mist-maker backpack shouting with her hands in the air, the creatures around her turned and began to clap and cheer.

"SHE'S HERE!" Odge cried triumphantly, scaling a rock to address the crowd. "I'VE BROUGHT HER HOME!"

A skinny young man with a mop of brown

hair pushed his way through the crowds. Lina was confused by his appearance—he was taller than the average teenage boy, and perhaps his eyes were a little bluer than most, but, aside from that, he was entirely human, from what she could see. Apart from her, he seemed to be the only human there.

He came to a stop in front of them and gave Odge a big hug. "I'm so glad you're all right, Gribs. We expected you earlier than this, and I got worried." He looked around hopefully. "Where's Hans?"

"Slight problem with the quantities of fernseed," Odge said, just as Ray began to un-vanish behind her.

The boy stumbled backward. "Is that . . . Ray? Odge, what did you *do to him*?"

Odge shifted her feet awkwardly. "I . . . He heard music . . . The piano . . . We had cake . . . But look how much more cuddly he is now!"

Lina could tell Ben was fond of Odge, because he couldn't help but smile.

"And anyway," Odge went on, "I brought the mistmaker master, didn't I?"

Ben looked to the brollachan entrance. "Where is the mistmaker master? Was she far behind you?"

"She's here," Odge said in a tone that suggested she thought him quite mad.

Ben looked at Lina and then back to Odge again. "I don't want to be rude, but there's no way that's the mistmaker master."

Odge sighed impatiently. "She has a mistmaker backpack, and she was on the platform. There's no way someone who *wasn't* the mistmaker master would be on the platform at the time we agreed, wearing a mistmaker backpack!"

"She speaks so badly to the Prince," a witch whispered to another, their hair ablaze.

The Prince, Lina thought. Of course. He was the one Magdelena had mentioned—the prince Odge had saved.

"Odge," Ben said, pulling the hag aside, though still very much in earshot of Lina. "She's a *child*. The mistmaker master is not a child. She's a one-hundred-and-one-year-old creature."

"Lina could be one hundred and one," Odge protested. "I haven't asked her age—it's rude. And, anyway, some people age well, you know."

"I'm . . . I'm not," Lina said.

"Hang on, Lina," Odge said. "I just need to speak to Ben."

"No, Odge. Listen—I'm sorry, but I have

been trying to tell you. I'm not . . . I'm not—"

Ben turned to Lina. "It's all right—I'm Ben, and I am the prince of this island, and I am now officially in charge, as of a few days ago when my parents were banished back to the human world by the harpies."

"He thinks he's in charge," Odge whispered. "But everyone knows I'm the one who makes the decisions. The good ones, anyway."

"My parents were sent to London and told never to return," Ben went on, "and I went into hiding here in the Undermist. The harpies don't know I'm still on the Island. The night the gump opened, the harpies attacked and seized power, and that's when the mistmaker creatures began getting sick. They have almost completely stopped producing mist, and it's the mist that keeps our island protected."

"So, the harpies are killing the Island," Odge added. "And we have until tomorrow night when the gump closes to stop them."

Ben sighed. "We've been trying to stop the harpies in any way we can, but our numbers have been dwindling fast. Many creatures have been thrown out through the gump, and many more are fleeing." As he spoke, he guided Lina to a rocky cave where an old witch was using an even older fairy like a pen to draw on the wall. Glistening slug-like trails formed what looked like a blueprint plan.

"This is where we plan and record resistance activities," Ben said as the witch and fairy scrawled FAILED next to everything. "And where we list plans that have so far failed."

Lina could see that on the second day of the takeover, Odge had gone to seek the help of the mutant mermaids to stop the harpies.

"We lost because we couldn't get the harpies into the sea, so the mermaids could only splash them from afar," Ben said.

"I think it *annoyed* them, though," Odge argued. "Their handbags got wet. It's a small victory."

Ben forced a smile and patted the neighboring section of the wall. "The next day, the mistmakers started growing weaker. We tried everything to make them better—I whistled tunes and played the flute for hours, because that usually makes the mist pour out of them, but it didn't work. That same day, the harpies set their sights on the mountains and defeated our troll friends up there."

Odge groaned. "That one wasn't my fault.

I had no idea ogres and trolls were so severely scared of sharp talons."

Lina noticed the witch and fairy had written USELESS TROLLS next to that one.

"By the seventh day, Odge and I had fallen out," Ben said. "I was getting really worried about the mistmakers and the fact that if the gump closed when my parents were in the human world it would be years before I saw them again. Odge had no sympathy for me and said I was giving up."

"You *were* giving up. It was infuriating."

The writing witch and fairy turned slowly to face them.

"No," Ben said quickly. "Don't record that."

"What happened yesterday?" Lina asked, running her hand over a drawing of a swirling gump and crying creatures.

"That's when the harpies went full steam ahead on evicting the magical creatures," Ben said sadly. "Our friends were vanishing through the gump, the mistmakers were fading fast, and we couldn't think of any way to defeat the flying harpies. Then I had a thought—perhaps fixing the mistmakers was the key to beating them. Those evil creatures fly high in battle, but if the mistmakers were better at producing mist it would be so cloudy that they wouldn't be able to see! We'd have an advantage—they'd be flying blind. I'm convinced we have to make the mistmakers better to defeat the harpies—"

"And that's exactly why *I* make the decisions," Odge butted in. "I told Ben I disagreed with him. I think the mistmakers are so sad about what's happening that they're giving up, just like Ben. This island has become horrible under the harpies' rule, and they no longer want to protect it, so they've stopped producing mist. And because they've stopped producing mist they're dying— and our island is dying with them. The only way to help them is to defeat the harpies. If we make this island good again before the gump closes tomorrow night, the mistmakers will be restored to their former glory. Look how happy Ray was off the Island in Vienna! He puffed up to the size of a furry uncle!"

"I told Odge, somewhat crossly," Ben said, his voice losing its measured tone, "that she could very well be right, but she couldn't be certain— she wasn't an *expert*."

"So I wrote to you, Lina—an *expert*—and said I would meet you the next morning at Vienna

Central Station," Odge said. "I didn't like seeing Ben so sad, but also I really wanted to prove that I'm right."

"So you went all the way to Vienna to win an argument?" said Lina, who couldn't really see what they were arguing about at all.

"Of course," Odge replied.

"I'm in hiding, or else I'd have met you myself," Ben said.

"So, the big question is, do we need to save the mistmakers to defeat the harpies? Or do we need to defeat the harpies to save the mistmakers? We agreed that the mistmaker master would guide us," Odge explained.

They both stared at Lina.

"But," Ben said slowly, "I'm guessing what you've been trying to tell Odge is you're not the mistmaker master at all?"

Lina pulled awkwardly on her jumper. "I did try to say. But I got distracted by the procession of magical creatures in the hotel—oh, and by the cake before that, and the giant mistmaker and the ghost rat, and then suddenly I was invisible and in a gump! And now I'm here."

"WRONG ONE!" the writing witch shouted, and she and the fairy quickly got to work drawing the latest failure on the wall.

Lina turned slowly to see Odge was standing with her jaw practically on the floor in shock.

"Not *again*," she finally said.

"Again?" Lina whispered to Ben. "This has happened before?"

"Mistaken identity is Odge's specialty," Ben said with a soft smile.

Odge began hitting her head against a brollachan, making a squelching noise in perfect harmony with her screaming. She stopped and began pacing instead, then stood on something that made her stop.

"Great," she groaned, lifting up a tiny, perfectly round stone. It glistened, and through a tiny crack a weird liquid dribbled onto the floor.

"Cor's enchantment," Ben said with a smile. "He was our wizard friend. He was very old and sadly passed away last year. But he left enchantments for us all across the Island—little things to remember him by."

The enchantment cast a stormy raincloud above the hag's head, and rain began beating down on her. She clenched her fists in frustration.

"It matches your mood," Ben joked. "That's such a Cor joke."

"I just wasted a day hanging out in Vienna with an ordinary kid. We're back to square one."

Odge let out a long howl and then went back to hitting her head on the jelly brollachans.

Ben smiled at Lina. She could tell he was disappointed and worried, but he was clearly kind, so it probably hadn't even crossed his mind to be horrible to her because of it.

"I can help," Lina said, wanting desperately to do something good. "I love magic and magical creatures, and I may not be the mistmaker master, but I am a quick thinker—I came up with the solution for getting Ray back here. I also have a handy backpack."

"How did you know what the mistmakers look like?" Ben asked curiously as he eyed the mistmaker backpack.

"Mistmaker backpack," a rock monster whispered.

Lina puffed up her chest proudly. "I imagined them."

"Well, in that case, you are very welcome here," Ben said with a smile. "Everything happens for a reason—I really believe that—and this island speaks to us when we take the time to listen. It's sent you to us, and that must mean something."

Squelch, scream, squelch, scream.

Lina wasn't so sure.

CHAPTER SIX

NETTY PRUDDLE

THE HARPIES believed that they had been the first magical creatures to live on Mist, and so that meant it belonged to them. Under their new regime, most creatures were unwelcome on the Island, but there were a few exceptions. The swamp fairies, for example, were needed to form an army, and so they were allowed to stay. But almost every other magical creature was banished and their homes taken. They were told never to return to the Island, because it was never theirs in the first place.

As a last-minute decision, the harpies decided to keep the hags too, because they believed their large hands would be good for chores, but that was before they'd seen them try to make a frilly harpy bed.

Netty Pruddle the hag struggled to tuck in

the final ruffled corner, then stood back, her eyes closed, awaiting the verdict. Four other beds were lined up in the room, and four other hags—Grunty, Esmergrotsla, Twitlee, and Gordon—stood beside them, looking equally nervous.

They were participating in a grueling competition to become the handmaid to the new harpy queen. Of course, Netty had no intention of *actually* being a handmaid; she was working undercover for the resistance. Or, at least, she was trying to.

"NETTY, THIS IS *TERRIBLE* WORK!" Mrs. Smith, the harpy queen, roared, making Netty's many boils wobble. "WHERE ARE THE DELICATE FOLDS I ASKED FOR? THE CREASE-LESS SURFACE? THE PLUMP PILLOW?"

Netty bent double and prodded the pillow with her finger in the hope that it might plump it.

The three other important harpies—Miss Green, Miss Brown, and Miss Witherspoon—grinned smugly.

Netty gritted her mammoth teeth, thinking of her friend Odge. *It'll be fine*, Odge had said. *You'll be able to gather important information*, Odge had said. *Netty, you can't lose*, Odge had said. Odge had the easy job—she was off having a great time in

Vienna collecting the mistmaker master, while Netty was stuck on a mountain making frilly beds for half-human, half-bird women with an attitude problem.

"GORDON, YOUR BED-MAKING IS THE WORST!" Mrs. Smith spat, grabbing the poor hag with her talons and guiding him toward the window.

Netty heard a sickening thud followed by Gordon's heavy hag footsteps stomping off down the rocky mountains to freedom. Oh, how she wished she were Gordon in that moment. As she daydreamed, her long eyelashes suddenly flashed blue (which meant wet weather was on the way), just as rain began lashing down outside.

"CAN SOMEONE PLEASE DISPOSE OF THIS I WENT TO HANS-OME CHEESES AND BOUGHT THIS CHEESE PLAQUE," Mrs. Smith roared, kicking it with her talon straight at Netty's face. "WE'LL DECIDE WHO WINS THE FINAL ROUND WHEN WE SEE HOW YOU'VE DONE WITH MY SHOPPING LISTS." And with that, she flew out of the room, leaving a foul-smelling trail as she went.

The harpies had originally lived in Central Mist, but when they seized power and threw out all the ogres and trolls, they decided to take over their houses. To anyone other than a troll, a troll's mountain home was a mansion.

Netty and the others had been tasked with redecorating the rock mansions to make them harpy-appropriate. First, they had thrown out all the chunky troll furniture—luckily there was a huge crack in the mountain with an endless drop, which was a perfect place to dispose of giant furniture.

Then they got to work on the shopping lists. Netty had ordered nineteen solid-gold perches (harpies like to perch), four long, thin mirrors (which had all shattered during one of Mrs. Smith's particularly shrill rants), four long beds (which she could not make to the standards demanded by the harpies), two thousand hair curlers, a trunk full of handbags from Evil Clutches, and some foul-smelling makeup from Gutsface Inc.

"I give up," Esmergrotsla groaned. Her armpit hair was wilting from the stress of the bed-making.

Grunty and Twitlee nodded along with her.

"Let's all go," Grunty said. "I hear there's a resistance, led by Odge Gribble, and they are hiding somewhere on the Island. We can join them if we can find them."

Netty frowned. "I can't. I have to stay here—it's important. But the others are hidden in the tunnels under Center Mist—they call it Undermist. Look out for the brollachans, and you'll find the hidden entrance."

The three hags made for the door.

"Good luck, Netty," Grunty whispered over her shoulder.

Netty watched from the window as they all made their escape, scuttling off down the mountain.

"Psst," came a voice, distracting Netty from her thoughts of freedom. "Psst. Are you Netty?"

Netty turned to see a kind-looking ghost woman hovering in the corner of the room. She was holding a small scrap of paper and moving it left and right, looking from it to Netty and back again.

"I suppose it looks a bit like you," the ghost mumbled.

Netty stomped over and took the piece of paper. "May I?" she asked.

The ghost nodded.

Netty scrunched up her warty face when she saw it. She recognized the artist instantly as Odge. She was a wonderful hag and friend, but a truly awful artist—though she had obviously tried to draw a picture of Netty so the ghost could identify her, which was smart.

"It looks like a lumpy potato in a skirt," Netty said.

"I've come to collect your message," the ghost whispered with a rebellious-looking smile. "I'm Miriam Hughes-Hughes. I haunt the gump on Platform Thirteen of King's Cross Station, London. I ANNOUNCE HOW LATE THE TRAINS ARE GOING TO BE IN THIS ANNOUNCER VOICE I'M DOING RIGHT NOW."

"Shh," Netty begged. "They'll hear you."

"*Sorry,*" Miriam Hughes-Hughes mouthed.

"Thank you for coming all this way, Miriam Hughes-Hughes. I'm sure you must be using valuable haunting time to be here."

"Not at all," Miriam Hughes-Hughes said, clearly enjoying Netty's gratitude. "I barely haunt at all these days—kids see so many ghosts on TV that they think I'm nothing more than some sort of high-tech advertisement for a retirement home. They're more scared of a flock of panicking pigeons. You know, when they go *WHOOSH* in your face? Sometimes I stomp my foot at just the right moment to send the pigeons soaring and get a sort of secondhand scare out of them, but that's about as good as it gets these days. And, anyway, I am happy to help with the rebellion. I've never liked harpies—they were always very rude if they went through my gump. And rudeness is as unhelpful as a train controller trapped in a toilet."

Netty was confused at the last bit.

"That's a little train-controller humor for you. I've been trying my hand at it recently, you see."

"Well, you are most appreciated, Miriam Hughes-Hughes. A crucial part of this operation. And I'm glad you managed to pick me out from all the other hag servants based on this potato drawing from Odge."

"I thought it looked more like a fat toe," Miriam Hughes-Hughes mused. "But yes—I am glad to have found you. Now, what message should I deliver?"

"Please tell Odge," Netty whispered, looking around to check the coast was clear, "that I'm *in*. I'm going to get the handmaid job—by default, because everyone else quit. Oh, and also, I am working on a plan that involves hair rollers."

A bead of sweat ran down Miriam Hughes-Hughes's face as she tried to write it all down on the back of the drawing. She flashed Netty a smile, told her to stay safe, and then floated off out the window.

Netty slumped on one of the beds and sighed, as she'd completely squashed it.

"NETTY!" she heard Mrs. Smith roar. "YOU WIN! YOU'RE THE CHIEF HANDMAID. YOUR FIRST TASK IS TO HELP US FIND YOUR ESCAPED FRIENDS! ALSO, I NEED HAIR ROLLERS!"

"COMING!" Netty shouted back, before whispering to herself, "We will defeat you." She skipped out of the room, her boils jiggling as she went.

"Interesting conversation," one of the rocks on the wall muttered to the other.

"Yes, interesting—that message and the ghost," said another, about ten hag steps from the house.

"Fascinating hag spy," said another, about twenty-nine hag jumps from the house.

"News travels fast in these parts," said another rock, on which the Central Mist sign was carved.

That was the problem with the Island of Mist: rock monsters could be found everywhere—and they were always talking . . .

CHAPTER SEVEN

THE LITTLE LAKE OF MIST

L INA TOOK in the sights of Undermist as
Ben guided them to a spot to eat.

Trolls crouched in the cramped tunnels reading books with type as long as Lina's face. Swamp fairies soaked their feet in bubbling rock pools next to old wizards making rocks glide about in pretty formations.

Ben took a left down a narrow tunnel filled with a particularly potent smell and came to a halt in a cave filled with cauldrons and witches of every age. When the witches saw them, they began cackling madly, as if someone had just switched them on.

Ray the mistmaker was slowly beginning to shrink as Lina guided him carefully by the paw to catch up with the others. She'd tried whistling, hoping the music would work, but it didn't. He flopped about like a wilting leaf, and all Lina wanted to do was make him feel better.

Odge hadn't spoken the whole way there, but did occasionally kick herself and yelp—a self-inflicted punishment for mistaking a young girl for the mistmaker master.

"Gribs, we'll figure it out," Ben said kindly to Odge. "And look—Ray is wilting again. I think you're right. The mistmakers are sad about the Island, and it's making them ill. They exist to protect our island, but without an island worth protecting, they're fading. We need to stop the harpies to save them—I should've just listened to you."

Odge ignored him and held up three fingers to a witch, who nodded. Lina looked up just as three cauldrons appeared above their heads and tipped up and over, pouring a hot and sticky liquid over her head.

She screamed, but no sound came out, as if the gloop had swallowed it up. She felt it ooze across her face, moving in all directions as if someone were smearing her with it. When the gloop eventually cleared, and she looked around, she could see they weren't in the cave anymore but somewhere completely different.

"We're still in the cave," Odge said with a smile. It was the first thing she had said to Lina since finding out she wasn't the mistmaker master, and Lina was relieved not to detect any resentment in her voice. "The potions just make it a little more exciting. It can be a bit dull hiding in an underground tunnel."

All around Lina, trolls danced on polished black floors that stretched out under painted vaulted ceilings strung with dancing toads on tightropes. A band of fairies hovered overhead, singing too softly to be heard properly over the roar of chatter. Efficient witch waiters glided from table to table, magically making orders appear.

"MENU?" one asked, plonking down a little maggot on the table.

Lina stared blankly at it.

"You need to tell it what you want," Ben explained. "I was confused by this magic when I came here too! It's not like a menu we'd find in the human world; it's a *MENU*. It stands for *Maggot Everything Now, Urgently*. Whisper something you'd like."

Lina felt silly. She leaned in close to the maggot and said, "Chocolate bar."

The maggot did a little wiggle as the witch tipped her hat, and, just like that, the maggot vomited up a chocolate bar.

Lina picked it up and inspected it—it was exactly the one she had been thinking of, right down to the emerald-green wrapper.

Odge ordered a large cheese pie and a chocolate coin with her face on it, and Ben went for a milkshake, which was particularly horrible to see a maggot vomit up.

"Where are your parents living in London?" Lina asked. "If you're the Prince, then they must be the King and Queen. Are they staying at a royal palace?"

"A school canteen," Ben said. "Some of the witches beyond the gump got them temporary jobs. They're human, so it's easy for them to go unnoticed."

"I've been thinking," Lina said. "I could go back to Vienna and find the mistmaker master for you."

Ben shook his head. "No—the mistmaker master will be spooked now. They say she rarely comes out of hiding. For some reason, she doesn't want anyone to know she's the mistmaker master. Odge wrote the letter and hoped she'd be there to meet her, but who knows—maybe she never came. If she did, and Odge didn't meet her, there will be no convincing her to meet again."

Odge stared up at the tightrope-walking toads and exhaled loudly. "I ruined everything."

"Well, then I will help stop the harpies," Lina said, struggling to bite through her solid chocolate bar. "How many of them are there?"

"Well," Ben said, "there are the main four. Mrs. Smith is the boss—she always has been. The other three do what she says. They're virtually identical, although you can tell which one Miss Green is because of the way she flies. She ate one of the enchantments Cor left around the Island, and now she can only fly backward. There was a fifth, a Miss Jones, but she disappeared after the gump opened, and we haven't seen her since."

"I thought I saw her in Vienna," Odge said, more to herself than the others. "But I was wrong."

"Aside from them," Ben went on, "there are about a hundred other less important harpies who don't seem to do much now they've got their troll mansions. Mrs. Smith is the one to defeat— she is the ringleader."

"So," Lina said, "we have two days until the closing of the gump to defeat evil Mrs. Smith and get all the banished magical creatures—and Ben's

parents—back home. Then there won't be any-
body shut out anymore, so the mistmakers will
be happy again, and the Island will be saved."

Odge nodded in agreement. "You can stay and
help, and I hope we can do it. But no matter what
happens, at the closing of the gump, we must get
you home safely."

"But we'll have to disguise you before we even
think about leaving Undermist," Ben added. "The
harpies hate almost all creatures that aren't like
them, but they hate humans most of all. What is
important to me is that we keep you safe."

"I've got some options," a witch said, dumping
various costume bits at Lina's feet. "My favorite is the troll baby, or possibly the giant swamp
fairy . . . Your choice though!"

"Ooh, are they magic?" Lina asked hopefully.

The witch looked annoyed, as if people expected
her to be magic all the time. "Yes," she said,
leaning closer to Lina. "It's called the magic of
sewing."

Lina smiled and lifted the costume sitting
limply on the top of the pile. It was a spiky green
wig attached to some bright orange overalls. She
fished a little dummy made out of rock from the
pocket.

"You know, I don't think she's big enough to be a troll baby," Odge said, sounding entirely serious.

Ben nodded in agreement, lifting some fake fairy wings. "And too big to be a giant fairy."

"What's this one?" Lina asked, lifting the third and final option from the floor.

"It's perfect," Odge said with a smile. "You'll be safe wearing that."

It turned out rock-monster costumes were surprisingly heavy—something Lina was learning as she tried to balance on the barstool while disguised as one.

"So, if there's ever any danger, just drop like a rock and stay very still," Odge said. "It's perfect."

Lina was hoping she'd be dressed as one of the more magical of Mist's characters—a baby troll or giant fairy would've been much more exciting than a rock monster.

One of the witch waiters picked up Lina's mistmaker backpack and looped it onto the rock. "There you go, human girl."

Lina was about to suggest they try another costume option—*any* other costume option—

when the ghost of a woman came sailing into the cave. She floated straight through Lina, and the whole room began to shrink, the fairy band stopped playing and vanished with a pop, and before Lina could blink she was back in the dark, cramped underground cave with nothing but the witches stirring their big cauldrons.

"Ghosts break most potions," Odge explained to Lina. "They contaminate them."

Miriam Hughes-Hughes looked offended. "Well, I'm sorry for interrupting your fantasy lunch burped up by magic maggots, but I bring news from the big toe . . . I mean the potato . . . I mean Netty. And a letter from your parents, Ben."

"Netty Pruddle!" Lina cried, remembering the name from the journey in Magdelena's carriage. "The hag undercover at the harpy mansion! What news? Is it good?"

"Who is this?" Miriam Hughes-Hughes said.

"This is Lina," Ben said. "She's a human who came here by accident, but she's staying for a while to help us. Then she'll need to go back home to her parents."

"My parents!" Lina said, suddenly feeling a rush of guilt. "They'll be wondering where I am."

Miriam Hughes-Hughes puffed up her chest. "I shall deliver a message to them. I'll tell them you will be home soon."

"Oh, Miriam Hughes-Hughes, I'm not sure . . ." Ben began, knowing full well a human would find little comfort in a message delivered by ghost.

"It is no trouble, dear Prince. Any friend of yours is a friend of mine. I'll go now—I insist." And then she sailed off grandly through a wall before anyone could stop her.

Ben sighed. "Maybe your parents will enjoy her visit . . ."

Lina nodded politely, knowing full well they almost certainly would not.

"HAIR ROLLERS?" Odge suddenly shouted. She waved Netty's letter above her head. "HAIR ROLLERS!"

"What does that mean?" Lina whispered to Ben.

Ben shrugged.

"She's gone and done it—she's the chief hand-maid to the harpies," Odge said, talking fast. "But she's also planning some sort of plot involving hair rollers. I told her to spy only—no plots. But you know what Netty is like."

"What *is* Netty like?" Lina whispered to Ben.

"Clumsy," Ben whispered back as Odge paced the room.

"We can't let her do anything stupid," Odge said.

"A plan to stop some evil harpies with hair rollers doesn't sound stupid," Lina lied.

Odge collapsed on one of the cauldrons and dunked her head in it. When she came back up, she had a dozy grin on her face. "Ah, that potion takes you to the Haglands in the summertime."

Ben bent down, wiped the gloop from her face, and grabbed her shoulders. "Gribs, you don't have time for trips to the beach."

"*I know*," Odge snapped. It was the first time Lina had seen her angry at anyone other than herself. "*I* went to get the mistmaker master, did I not?"

Ben clearly didn't dare to say anything.

"Do you have any more ideas to stop them?" Lina interrupted.

"At the moment, we don't have a plan at all," Ben whispered.

Odge pinched the bridge of her nose and paced the room, her blue boots crunching the rocky ground as she went.

"The problem is the harpies have retreated to the mountains," Ben explained to Lina.

"Why don't we head to the mountains, then," Lina said, still dressed as a rock.

"I have considered it," Odge said. "But I was hoping Netty would be able to report on their movements. They won't always stay up there—they'll move around. Ben is right—when they fly, they are almost impossible to stop. Our only hope now is to somehow ambush them when they're on the ground. But for a plan like that, we need the insider information from Netty. We need to know exactly where they will be and when."

"What if they came right here?" Lina said, an idea forming. "And we were ready for them."

"To Central Mist?" Odge said with a laugh. "Oh, Lina, they won't do that. They destroyed the palace and the whole town square; it's a wreck, and they hate a mess. No, they'll wait until the gumps close, and then—knowing all the creatures they hate are on the other side of them—they'll rebuild Mist exactly the way they want it to be. Probably with a lot of harpy statues, those arrogant birds."

"But I think I know what would get them to come flying back here," Lina said with a smile.

She meant herself—the human girl who had managed to get through the gump. They could use her as bait! It would be a wonderful solution to an awful problem, and Lina would finally be useful. They could use her to tempt the harpies— they would surely be curious as to why their security system had failed! And they hated humans. It was a brilliant plan.

"There is one person," Lina continued, giddy with excitement and adventure, "who would tempt them here."

Ben stepped forward. "A prince," he said bravely. "They'll come if they know I'm here."

Lina tried to interrupt, but it was no good.

"Ben, that might just work," Odge said.

"No—*me!*" Lina cried, trying to jump up and down, but the rock costume was too restrictive. "I am the one. I honestly don't mind doing—"

Odge put her arms round Lina and Ben. "We'll have the rebellion team rig some traps in Central Mist, then we'll send Ben out, and when the harpies come for him—*BOOM!* The traps will catch them. They won't be able to fly off—we'll have the advantage. We can't fail."

Lina hoped with all her heart that Odge was right . . .

CHAPTER SEVEN 1/2

THE P.S.

Dearest Ben,

We are coping well here at the school but missing you terribly. The canteen witches have been very kind and given us their jobs while they take a few days off to visit a theme park. Apparently a new roller coaster has just opened. The witches may be magic, but roller coasters absolutely astound them.

I must say, getting the hang of human things is tricky after a lifetime on Mist. My job is to deep-fat fry things, and I am rather good at it now, if I do say so myself. I've done chips, fish, and homework jotters. Your father is on washing-up duty, which is a lot more difficult here in the canteen.

He's been doing plates and cups and all the gym kits, which the kids tell us is definitely the responsibility of the canteen staff. Oh, and a squirrel.

The head teacher is so incredibly lovely and always asking us if we're feeling all right and if we need our "heads checked," which is presumably her area of expertise, given her job title.

All in all, this experience has been wonderful, though I am plagued with constant worry for our island and especially our dear mistmakers. I am so proud of you for all that you are doing to help, and our steadfast and wonderful Odge too. But please, dear Ben, do be careful. The harpies' tricks and talons are not to be taken lightly, and I do not want you doing anything that could put you in harm's way. You must not let them find out you're still there.

We think of you always and await your arrival through the gump. Come soon, Ben.

Love,
Mother and Fa
P.S. Mistma er Mis es visit

The last section of the letter had been so thoroughly deep-fat fried that the final sentences were too crispy to read. They crumbled to nothing before anyone even noticed they were there, which was unfortunate, because there was a very important P.S. right at the bottom.

CHAPTER EIGHT

THE ROCK MONSTERS

NETTY PRUDDLE tiptoed along the corridor in the old troll house and heaved her way up the giant stone steps. They were large even for a sizable hag, and she had to hurl herself up with both arms and flip herself over in order to make it. She understood now why piddly little humans always described walking up stairs as "climbing" them—it really was a climb when one was so small compared to the stairs.

In Mrs. Smith's bathroom, she found the stash of hair rollers. She reached into the pocket of her apron and rummaged around, pulling out identical ones and replacing them one at a time.

"NETTY!" came a screech, making the hag jolt.

She raised her head slowly, sneaking a peek out the window. She could see Mrs. Smith and the other three flying fast toward the house.

"NETTY!" Mrs. Smith screeched again, making the windows shatter.

Netty hastily picked up the last of the hair rollers and stuffed them in her apron. She could hear the harpies flying up the stairwell, their talons scraping the steps as they went. With trembling hands she lined up the remaining rollers just as Mrs. Smith kicked open the door. The harpy flung her handbag across the room and straight out the broken window, stopping and staring in disbelief as it soared down the mountain and toppled a hag standing by a tree.

"Netty," she snapped. "I can't believe you broke the window!"

"Actually, Mrs. Smith, that was you when you screech—"

The harpy grabbed the hag's lips to *shh* her. "Be careful, hag"—she shook her head—"that sounded like rebellion to me."

Netty tried to back away, but the talons dug deeper.

Mrs. Smith's harpy friends flew into the room.

"Did you ask her? I bet she knows," Miss Witherspoon hissed as the others whispered excitedly.

"Knows what?" Netty asked quietly as soon as Mrs. Smith eased her grip.

"We went down to the swamp to have a word with our new swamp-fairy army," Mrs. Smith said, flying in circles round Netty's head and making her feel dizzy. "And we bumped into a little rock monster who had something *fascinating* to say."

Netty gulped. Could a rock monster know she was a secret spy? Did they know about her plan with the hair rollers? Her gaze instinctively shifted to them neatly lined up on the table. She quickly squeezed her eyes shut, realizing she might be giving the plan away. A bead of sweat dribbled down her boil-covered face.

"Netty," Mrs. Smith whispered. "You're a very famous hag, aren't you? Famous for your beauty?"

Netty nodded.

"You've graced the covers of hag magazines and modeled hag clothes?"

Netty nodded again, keeping her eyes squeezed shut so she didn't look at the hair rollers again.

"You're a popular hag, aren't you? You know lots of other hags. In fact, I bet there's not a hag on the Island that you don't know."

Sweat cascaded down Netty's face as if it were a boil-infested waterfall.

"*You* know Odge Gribble, the one we believe is plotting a rebellion."

Netty rolled her head back and paused, as if searching the recesses of her brain for an Odge. "Who?" she said, her voice shaking. "Splodge?"

"I think we all know you know Odge Gribble," Mrs. Smith said impatiently, clicking her fingers to summon Miss Witherspoon, who produced a piece of paper, which Mrs. Smith inspected closely. "You were due to attend Mist University together. You applied to be roommates because, and I am quoting, *We've known each other forever and are the best of friends.*"

In that moment, Netty was pretty certain she was going to be killed. Odge did have a habit of getting her into the most dire situations, like all those times she wrote letters pretending to be her, using her "Netty the Hag"-branded stationery.

Dear Mutant Mermaids,

I've got to squeeze my boils, and I was wondering if you'd mind if I squeeze them into your beloved lagoon? It won't take long, and I'm positive you'll be delighted with the gooey results.

Your pus-filled hag friend,
Netty

Netty had to take the long route into town after that to avoid being splashed aggressively by the mutant mermaids.

Dear Ben,

   Netty here. Just wanted to say how much I adore your eyebrows. May I borrow them?
                              Yours less-hairily,
                              Netty

Ever since the joke letter, Ben always held on to his eyebrows when he saw Netty coming, as if she might rip one off and try it on.

"Hellloooo?" Mrs. Smith snapped, clapping in Netty's face. "Is the hag still there?"

Netty shook her head, leaving the daydream behind to return to the dark, damp troll mansion.

"You see, the rock monster spoke of a human— a young girl with a mistmaker backpack."

Netty opened her eyes excitedly. "I know nothing about a human girl with a mistmaker backpack," she said, and that was the truth. One of her face boils burst from the relief of it all, sending a spray of pus onto Mrs. Smith's spindly nose.

"The rock monsters seemed to think she wasn't alone. They saw her with a hag."

Netty bit her lip, worried for a second that perhaps she had befriended a human girl with a mistmaker backpack and had just forgotten. She searched every corner of her brain before concluding, "It *definitely* wasn't me!"

"Of course it wasn't you, idiot," Mrs. Smith snapped. "It was that troublemaker, Odge. She's your friend, is she not?"

"She is not," Netty lied.

"What would she want with a young human girl with a mistmaker backpack?" Mrs. Smith inquired, leaning so close to Netty that her boils retreated into her face in fear.

"Um . . . she might . . . want a friend . . . because I'm on your side now?"

Mrs. Smith rolled her eyes. "Don't be a fool, Netty. Odge brought that human through the gump for a reason, AND I WANT TO KNOW WHAT IT IS!" She grabbed Netty by the hair and guided her to the window. "If you were Odge, and you were hiding a human on this island, where would you go?"

Netty knew exactly where, but she was determined not to say.

The harpies weaved closer and stroked Netty's frazzled hair.

"Oh, pretty, big hag," Miss Witherspoon chimed torturously. "Did your hag friends all hide and leave you out?"

Mrs. Smith flew in front of her, pushing the other harpies aside. "You may not know Odge's hiding place, but what I really want to know, Netty Pruddle, is whose side are you on?"

Netty felt her breath quicken and tried desperately to slow it. She had a habit of hyperventilating when trying to lie. Her eyelashes flashed white, and outside, snow began to fall.

It distracted the harpies, allowing Netty a moment to compose herself.

"SNOW?" Mrs. Smith roared as her cronies flew fast to the window. "It hasn't snowed on Mist . . . ever. Did you do this, hag?"

"No," Netty said, breathing a sigh of relief. It was nice not to have to lie—she didn't start the snow, and that was the truth. Some hags could tell the weather with their eyelashes, but they couldn't control it. It was a common misconception among the less intelligent on Mist that hags were responsible for the weather—and they were often blamed for it, especially the rain. Netty couldn't count the number of times she'd had an angry umbrella hurled at her and been yelled at to turn the rain off.

"Peculiar," Mrs. Smith said, curling her talons in thought. "Very peculiar."

"Oh look," Miss Green said to Mrs. Smith. "Your hair rollers have arrived! May I borrow a few?"

Netty tried not to grin.

"Netty," Mrs. Smith said, her attention turning once again to the hag. "Why don't you take the rest of the day off. You've done very well for today, and I am satisfied that you are on our side."

She didn't need any encouragement—Netty was out the door in seconds. She had to warn the rebellion that the harpies were onto them. Odge must know—and fast. And whoever this little human was, she needed to get back through the gump; she was in severe danger! Netty charged down the mountain, feeling very smug that she'd fooled Mrs. Smith into thinking she had no idea where Odge was hiding.

The harpies hovered at the window, watching her run.

"And now we let her lead us straight to them," Mrs. Smith said with a satisfied smirk. "I want to know what that dratted human girl is doing here."

They clawed their way out the broken window and took to the skies.

CHAPTER NINE

THE HUMAN

IT WAS the rumble that they heard first. To Lina's untrained ears, it sounded sinister, like the furious stomps of something heavy and hungry, but Odge didn't look worried. In fact, her eyes lit up.

"I know those monstrous footsteps! Netty's here!" she cried, lifting her feet from the steaming fairy pool and pulling on her boots. She ran out of sight, leaving Lina, Ben, and Ray alone with the fairies.

"She'll be back," Ben said, twisting so he could peek down the corridor. "It's almost certainly not Netty; it's probably just a baby troll in a mood."

Ray wheezed and laid his fluffy head on Lina's lap. She stroked him and watched as the little fairies by the pool began fluttering about, saying the most foul swears Lina had ever heard in her life.

"Pretend you didn't hear that," Ben said with a wince. "Fairies are quite . . . rude."

"What's going on?" Lina whispered to one of them, being careful not to lean in too close. Being flower fairies, they were constantly met with the giant nostrils of those who wanted to sniff them, and Odge had warned Lina not to stick her nose anywhere near them.

"Snow," one of the fairies whispered, pointing at the pond while the others swore and screeched.

"And it seems they've been *drinking*," Ben said, throwing his hands in the air. "I'm sorry about them, Lina. They are quite irresponsible sometimes."

"No!" another squeaked, also pointing at the pond. "Look."

Lina gently moved Ray onto the feathery bed Ben had made for him and grabbed hold of the muddy rocks, pulling herself up and over the lip of the pond until her nose was practically dipped in it.

"Snow," the fairies all said at once.

Lina couldn't believe what she was seeing. In the pond, among the ripples and glinting rocks, was an image of the Island of Mist. Strong waves thrashed the town walls, spilling over into the rubble that had once been the shops of Center

Mist. And there—falling heavily, before landing and being swept away by the waves—was *snow.*

"Is that normal?" Lina asked.

"There is something very wrong with this island," Ben muttered, dusting off his trousers as he got up to take a look. "Without the mist from the mistmakers, the weather has been increasingly strange."

Lina was about to say they should peek outside, it could be a glitch in the fairies' magic, but she stopped when she spotted something emerging from the snow-soaked skies, flying faster and faster. She peered closer before recoiling in horror.

"Harpies!" Lina gasped as the fairies got distracted and started pulling each other's wings.

It was then that Odge came strolling back in, holding Netty's hand. "I'd recognize the sound of her thwomp-walk anywhere! Lina, this is my friend Netty—the one who's undercover at Mrs. Smith's house for us. Now, Netty, I'm glad you're here, because we've just hatched a plan. We're setting traps in Center Mist for the harpies! They should be ready by tomorrow. We'll lure them down and get them once and for all!"

Lina tried to speak. To shout, "*Harpies!*" To point at the pond. To let them know the harpies were already here—far too early and looking far too fierce. But panic whipped the noise away, and her arms were deadweights.

One of the tiny flower fairies cleared her throat with a delicate cough and helpfully shouted, "QUIET, YOU RATBAGS! THE HUMAN GIRL IS TRYING TO SPEAK!"

They all turned to Lina. "Harpies," she managed, her voice shaking. "Coming right for us."

"Impossible! How could they possibly know?" Odge cried.

Ben turned slowly to Netty. "Did the harpies follow you?"

Netty began to sweat. "They said I could have the rest of the day off."

"Harpies don't believe in days off for anyone but themselves!" Odge cried.

Netty's eyes grew wide when she spotted Lina's backpack. "THEY KNOW ABOUT THE LITTLE HUMAN! THEY'VE COME FOR HER!"

It was the last thing Lina heard before the roof above them exploded.

Mud and rock pummeled her as she grabbed Ray and desperately clawed her way along the crumbling corridors. She could just make out one of the flower fairies ahead of her.

"Wait!" she cried. "Please wait!" But the glowing

light of the flower fairy grew weaker and disappeared from view. Lina stopped, trembling in the dark.

Screams pierced her ears, but the air was too filled with dust to work out where they were coming from. Every so often, the cloak of a wizard or the wing of a fairy would whip past. She fought through the rubble and dust, pulling herself to her feet. Harpy cackles rang out around her.

"Odge?" she called. "Ben?"

She stumbled down the tunnel. Where once there had been witches and trolls and little wizards with braided beards, now there was no one. Not a single creature.

"It's all right. It's going to be all right," she whispered to Ray, though it was really to calm herself.

She slowly navigated her way over and around the rocks. Light flooded in from a hole in the ceiling, along with snow and spray from the waves. She wanted to stay put in the light and wait for Odge, but that's when she heard her—

"Over here!" came Odge's cry.

Only it wasn't Odge at all. The thing about harpies is they are incredibly skilled at imitating people's voices. They can also do some good animal noises, apart from cows. There's something about a *moo* that's beyond them.

Lina charged on until she reached the dark and dingy cave room they had been in earlier. Squinting, she could just make out the witches' cauldrons still bubbling away, but the witches themselves were long gone.

She walked slowly, whispering Odge's name. She was sure she had heard her voice coming from this very room.

The cauldrons creaked behind her, and a sinister shadow danced across the wall.

"Odge?" Lina whispered again, unaware of what was behind her.

She heard a scratching noise. It was a noise she'd heard before, when she'd first arrived in Mist. The noise that had echoed through the tunnel. The noise of a creature who wasn't flying but clawing. The noise of—

"A HARPY!" Lina screamed in fear as she whipped round.

But it was too late—all she saw was talons and then nothing at all.

The rebellion was a sorry sight. Witches were tied to emptied cauldrons, wizards were trying to hide in their beards, the flower fairies were trapped in glass jars, because everyone knows how vicious they can be, and poor Odge was being dragged by the ears by Miss Witherspoon and a backward-flying Miss Green. Next to her, Miss Brown and Mrs. Smith had a hold on Lina.

"She should've been wearing her rock monster disguise," Lina heard a witch whisper to another. "She took it off to dip her legs in the fairy pool, silly human."

Lina could feel her feet dragging along the ground, but the upper part of her body felt weightless. They were flying her somewhere, but had obviously decided it was more appropriately traumatic if they dragged her a bit too.

Her head was pounding, and her stomach was turning, but it was when it dawned on her that her arms were empty that she truly felt sick.

"Ray?" she tried to say, but it came out in a wobbled mumble.

"The child is speaking," Miss Witherspoon whispered to Miss Green. "Shall I offer to cut off its tongue?"

"No," Miss Green whispered back. "We need it to speak later. Mrs. Smith is very curious about why it is here. She fears it's a strange plan from Odge the hag. Humans are the worst of all."

"Even the small ones?"

"Especially the small ones, Miss Witherspoon."

Mrs. Smith and Miss Brown stopped and dropped Lina on a rock next to Odge. Miss Brown landed on Lina's head, digging her claws in, and Miss Green did the same to Odge, only backward. They were well and truly trapped—any escape would mean leaving without a head.

"I don't know where Ray is," Lina whispered desperately to Odge.

"It's talking again," Miss Witherspoon groaned. "I wonder if you cut off a tongue and sew it back on again later, does it still work?"

Miss Green pondered the question for a moment, tapping her claws deeper into Odge's head as she did. "You know what—I *don't know*. It sounds like something we would have to try in order to be certain about it."

Lina winced.

"THIS," Mrs. Smith roared, thankfully interrupting them, "IS WHAT HAPPENS WHEN YOU TRY TO OUTSMART ME! I HAVE BEEN IN CHARGE OF THE POLICE FORCE ON THIS ISLAND FOR MANY YEARS, AND THERE IS NO TUNNEL, NO CAVE, NO ROCK THAT I DO NOT KNOW. HIDE FROM ME,

AND I WILL FIND YOU! YOU WILL LEAVE THROUGH THE GUMP IMMEDIATELY, OR STAY AND FACE THE CONSEQUENCES."

She paused, breathing in deeply before announcing, "THE REBELLION IS OVER."

Hundreds of harpies hung above them, chattering excitedly. One of them dropped her handbag, and Lina watched it fall and hit Ben on the head. He straightened himself up.

"THE REBELLION WILL NEVER BE OVER!" he shouted as loudly as he could. Ben wasn't very good at shouting, and even when he tried his hardest it still sounded somewhat pleasant.

"WHO SPEAKS?" Mrs. Smith demanded. "WHO DARES TO SPEAK?" She turned to the other harpies. "Was that a shout or someone trying to sing?"

Ben stepped forward to some muffled cheers from the captured rebels. Lina watched him place Ray gently in one of the cauldrons. She breathed a sigh of relief. All she wanted to do was run over to the cauldron and scoop the mistmaker up, but now wasn't the time.

"WHO ARE YOU, YOU SWEET-SOUNDING HORROR?" Mrs. Smith demanded.

Miss Witherspoon whispered something

urgently to Mrs. Smith and received a glare for it.

"YES, OF COURSE I KNEW IT WAS THE PRINCE," she snapped, even though she clearly hadn't. A sinister grin spread greedily across her face.

Ben walked toward them, wobbling slightly as he went. Lina couldn't tell if he was losing his footing because of the debris or because he was shaking with fear.

"I wonder where his hideous parents are?" Miss Brown whispered to Miss Green. "Maybe they didn't go through the gump either."

"I escorted them myself," Mrs. Smith snapped. "I watched them go—to a world I knew wouldn't want them! At least they'll be able to blend in. I imagine the trolls and flower fairies and witches and other beasts will not have so much luck. They'll spend their lives hiding and lurking and never belonging!"

"Where's the fifth one?" Ben asked. He knew the harpies well—after all, they had once protected the royal family. "There's you, Mrs. Smith . . . Miss Witherspoon, Miss Brown, and Miss Green—but where's Miss Jones?"

"Who cares!" Mrs. Smith scoffed, even though she did care, very much. The five of them had been as thick as thieves since childhood—sisters in boldness, if not blood. They had ruled the harpy police force together, but when the gump opened, just after they had finally seized power, Miss Jones had vanished.

"Maybe *he* knows where she is," Miss Green seethed, unsticking her talons from Odge's head and flying over to Ben. Miss Brown released her grip on Lina and followed.

Now free from the harpies' talons, and with all eyes firmly fixed on Ben's distraction, Lina gave Odge a nod, and the two of them slid down the rock fast, scuttled through the crowds, and together they fished Ray out of the cauldron. Lina placed him gently in her backpack, and they made their way slowly around the crowd.

"We just need to get close enough to grab her," Odge said, rolling up her sleeves. "I hate that they can fly."

Lina gasped. "Grab Mrs. Smith?" Having seen the harpies in action and felt their talons, she wasn't keen to go anywhere near her again. "I don't think that's a good idea, Odge."

Odge turned to Lina and stared down at her. "Not a good idea?"

"Don't take it personally," Lina said quickly. "We need to be better prepared. Right now, we need to find a way to get Ben to safety, and then we need to hide."

Odge stared down at the rubble, all that remained of the tunnels of the Undermist. "*That* was the only hiding place."

"Where have they gone?" Miss Witherspoon squealed, pointing madly at the empty spot where Lina had sat moments earlier. "THEY'VE GONE! THE FOUL CHILD HAS GONE, AND SHE'S TAKEN ODGE GRIBBLE WITH HER!"

The crowd gasped. Mrs. Smith went black in the eyes and grabbed Ben. The other harpies stuck a talon each into his perfectly ironed jumper, and together the four of them hoisted him into the air.

Odge and Lina watched in despair as they flew up high out of reach.

"ODGE GRIBBLE!" Mrs. Smith's voice echoed through the snow, which had now turned to dagger-like sheets of slush, falling so fast that the world became a blur. "YOU CAN PLAY YOUR SILLY GAMES, BUT I THINK WE ALL KNOW I HAVE THE ONE THING THAT MEANS THE MOST TO YOU. TWO THINGS, ACTUALLY, WHEN YOU COUNT NETTY."

Lina peeked past a witch's hat to where the other, lesser harpies—all one hundred or so of them—were struggling to hoist Netty into the air.

"PLAY YOUR SILLY GAMES WITH THE FOUL CHILD, ODGE GRIBBLE," came Mrs. Smith's sinister voice. "WE'LL BE WAITING FOR YOU. BUT IN THE MEANTIME . . ."

There was a buzzing noise, and everyone's nose began to twitch.

"ROUND THEM UP!" Mrs. Smith cried as an army of swamp fairies descended from the crumbling old palace in a cloud of putrid smells. "TAKE WHAT REMAINS OF THE REBELLION AND KICK!

"THEM!

"OUT!"

Lina heard a familiar voice at her feet.

"Well, what are you waiting for? This is the bit when you run!"

She looked down to see a little ghost rat in pearls glaring up at her.

"Magdelena!" Lina cried. "What are you doing here?"

"What can I say? I like you, Lina, and I thought you might need a helping paw. Plus Netty's mother has flooded the hotel, and I cannot *stand* wet carpets."

"We have nowhere to hide," Lina said quickly. "Undermist is gone."

"Hmm," Magdelena said, ignoring the swamp fairies trying to grab at her ghost pearls.

Odge covered her face with her cloak and began batting the foul little things left and right.

A brollachan wobbled past with about a hundred other brollachans stuck to it.

"Well," Magdelena finally said as Lina tapped her foot impatiently, all the while hoping the suggestion would be worth the wait. "If the swamp fairies are busy being an army, that means no one is in Swampton."

"Swampton," Lina said to Odge as she pulled a swamp fairy from her cheek. "We need to go to Swampton."

"Oh no," Odge said, ducking to avoid a troll springing over the warring crowd. "Swampton smells."

Lina looked around in bewilderment. "I'd take smelly over mortal danger right now!"

"And, anyway," Odge said, "no one knows how to get in."

Magdelena laughed. "Are you the great Odge Gribble, or are you not?" She trotted off through the crowds. "It's this way, in case you're interested!"

"We'll get in," Lina said, grabbing Odge's

arm and pulling her fast through the rubble.

"How can you be so sure?" Odge shouted as they charged after Magdelena toward the shoreline.

"Because I want to be!" Lina shouted back.

They skidded to a halt in front of the thundering waves.

"Down here, quickly," Magdelena said.

Lina slipped along icy rocks as waves crashed down on them. Magdelena glided on effortlessly. Up ahead, Lina could just make out a cove. It sat opposite a similar cove on the other side of the half-moon-shaped beach.

Odge spotted Lina looking. "That cave over there is the entrance to the Platform Thirteen gump."

They both paused for a second and watched as magical beings were chucked into boats and sailed toward it—to be thrown through the gump and never allowed back.

"I worry about them in the human world," Odge said sadly.

The rocks under her feet flashed emerald green as if to tell them to hurry up. Lina forged on, occasionally glancing out to sea, where she spotted the feet of mutant mermaids breaking the surface of the waves. She blinked, wondering if she were imagining it, or if the talon prods to the head had done something to her vision.

"In here," Odge said, wrapping her arm round Lina and pulling her into a strangely tropical cave. It was covered in the most beautiful emerald leaves, mist rose from the floor, and the smell of sun-soaked sand filled the air. On the other side, carved out in a perfect circle, was an exit to what seemed to be a forest beyond.

Lina looked back at the icy spot they'd just come from. "Impossible!" she cried.

Magdelena stared at her. "You're surely not saying that to a ghost rat?"

CHAPTER TEN
THE SWAMP

LINA WADED through the wet grass at the edge of the swamp. It barely came up to her knees. Birds chirped in the trees, and a sticky, still air hung around them. As they walked through the gloopy water, Lina could feel things moving, brushing against her ankles and nibbling on her toes.

"Nothing dangerous in here," Magdelena assured her. "But I suppose I am dead."

"So if we hide here," Lina reasoned, "we'll be safe for a while, because the swamp fairies are all out and about and busy."

The swamp bubbled, making the fairy-sized leaves and lily pads move. Lina gulped.

"The swamp fairies live in a hidden place *within* the swamp called Swampton, and no one knows how to get in apart from them," Odge said.

"And from what I hear," Magdelena said, wrinkling her nose in disgust, "no one wants to find it—disgusting, smelly place it is."

"I bet *we* can find it," Lina said, pulling at reeds and pressing lily pads covered in bright swirls of purple and green. She waded out farther until she couldn't stand anymore.

"What's she doing?" she heard Odge whisper to Magdelena.

"Have you got any ideas, Magdelena?" Lina asked hopefully.

"Beats me, dear girl," Magdelena replied. "Do I look like a rat that's ever gone anywhere near a swamp?"

Lina shook her head no, because she knew that was the answer Magdelena wanted. To be perfectly honest, she'd always imagined rats would be right at home by a smelly swamp; she didn't for a second think they'd be wearing pearls and turning their tiny noses up at anything less than a five-star hotel.

"Ugh, Ben would probably be helpful," Odge said, hitting a lily pad in anger. "He's much better and more interested in this stuff than me. He'd be telling us all the names of plants and pointing at little worms we would've never spotted if it weren't for him." She picked up a worm and waved it to prove her point, until it bit her, and she accidentally flicked it at Lina.

Lina watched it bounce off a lily pad that looked a little different from the others. The water bubbled fast around it, as if there were some sort of creature lurking beneath it. And there was something about its color—the swirls were imperfect, and nature was usually a perfect painter. No, this one had been done by hand—tiny, tiny hands, by the look of it.

Lina swam over and tried to pick it up, but the gloopy water around the lily pad stuck to her skin like slime. She tried and tried to pull the lily pad up, but it wouldn't budge. Instead, the water seemed to grow even more sludgy and slimy until Lina didn't need to kick her legs to stay afloat— she was suspended and supported in it.

"That's either very promising or *very* worrying!" Odge said, giving the water a prod.

The ground began to rumble, and the birds fell silent. There was a weird *click*, and the lily pad sprang up into the air, and the gloopy water began to drain, taking Lina with it.

"LINA!" Odge cried, kneeling down and reaching out a hand.

But it was no good. No matter how much Lina stretched, Odge was too far away.

She sank lower and lower with the chunky water until she hit the seabed. The gunge seeped through thousands of tiny holes in the sides of the pond until there was nothing left but a scattering of lily pads and limp reeds.

"You did it!" Odge cheered, swinging her legs over the edge and landing with a thud next to Lina.

As soon as Odge hit the ground, the limp reeds scattered around them sprung to life, winding their way around the hag and the human.

"WHAT'S HAPPENING?" Lina cried as the reeds tightened around her.

The ground beneath them began to shudder.

"Is this supposed to—" Lina started, but the floor disappeared before she could finish. She somersaulted down with nothing to hold on to but the slippery reeds wrapped around her.

"Odge!" she cried. "ODGE!" She was terrified of heights, and it was very unnerving to feel the ground disappear beneath you.

Lina tried to catch sight of her friend, but they were both tumbling too fast, and all she could make out was a flash of black dress fabric and a blue boot heel.

She dropped down, the reeds tightening around her, threatening to snap. She felt herself ping back up, before dropping down again, hanging suspended above what looked like the smelliest and tiniest city she had ever seen.

Magdelena landed next to them. "Oh good— you're alive."

Lina untangled herself from the reeds and stood up on the swampy ground. When she looked back up, the swamp water was refilling above their heads. "We're *under* the swamp."

"So, this is Swampton," Odge said, ducking slightly so she could fit down one of the swampy streets. "Home of the swamp fairies."

Lina peered inside one of the buildings. They were made from rock and decorated with the same swirly lily pads that floated on the swamp's surface. Swamp goo oozed from the windows and dribbled down the sides. If Lina curled up, she'd just about fit inside an entire building. It smelled of untended public toilets. "So the whole town is completely empty?"

"Every single swamp fairy was recruited by the harpies to be the new police force on Mist. It was that or leave the Island forever, and the swamp fairies were scared of that," Odge said, tipping swamp goo out of her boots. "Apparently the harpies considered the wizards as their new police force, but wizards have got too much of a conscience, plus they don't smell. Harpies like to assault all your senses: high-pitched voices to hurt your ears, smells to attack your nose, and talons to go for your eyes."

"Do swamp fairies have talons like the harpies?" Lina asked.

"No, luckily," Odge said. "But they do have needle-sharp teeth. Horrible little things— although they are excellent chefs. Speaking of food, I say it's about time we found some."

Lina grinned. "And then we'll figure out how to save Ben and Netty and stop the harpies once and for all!"

"So it's just us now," Odge said glumly over a delicious gloopy meal eaten while squashed inside a small diner known as Sloppy Susan's.

With the entire rebellion being evicted and sent through the gumps, and her two friends captured by the harpies, it had dawned on Odge that she and Lina were the only ones who could stop the harpies. Given that Lina had only learned earlier that day that harpies definitely existed, it was not looking good.

Of course there was also Magdelena, but she was a ghost rat and not entirely reliable.

"So were you a magical rat when you were alive?" Lina asked, trying to lighten the mood.

"No," Magdelena said. "I was an imp. But I stole some pearls from a harpy—I am a demon, after all—so they cursed me to live as a rat for all of eternity. Joke's on them, though, because they picked a rat who lives in a five-star hotel."

"Well, that's . . ." Lina didn't know what to say.

"It's late," Odge said, squeezing her way out of the restaurant. "Let's find a place to sleep. Maybe an idea will come to us in our dreams."

"In your dreams," Magdelena couldn't resist saying.

And so they wriggled their way into a hotel. Although it was quite small, and they had to crawl through the entrance, the rooms were very grand by swamp-fairy standards. Lina used the bed as a pillow while, across the room at the other side, Odge mirrored her.

"This is all my fault!" Lina blurted out, just as Odge had clicked off the tiny lamp. Gooey swirls of light danced around the room, reflected from the swamp surface above.

"It's not your fault at all," Odge said kindly. "It's the harpies' fault."

Lina lay there in silence. "I can't leave knowing

the harpies haven't been stopped—if I go, you'll be all alone. That means we have almost no time left, and there's no time for sleeping!"

"Trust me, Lina," Odge said. "When you get a bit older, you realize just how magic sleep is."

"This time tomorrow, the gump will be closing," Lina said, jumping up and hitting her head.

Her backpack wriggled, and Ray climbed out. She scooped him up and cuddled him. "We *have* to stop the harpies—for everyone, but also for Ray."

Odge smiled a sad smile. "Ray really likes you."

"We can do it, Odge. We can!"

"I'm worried it's impossible, Lina. I don't want to think like that, but I can't help it now. The harpies have won."

"You saved a prince when you were about my age! I bet everyone thought that would be impossible!"

Odge groaned. "Well, there was a lot of luck involved."

"But you did it," Lina said. "Imagine if you had said from the very beginning that it was impossible that you, Odge Gribble, would be able to save the Prince, and then you just didn't try!

You wouldn't have saved him, even though you could have."

"This must be how Ben feels around me," Odge said, a smile breaking on her face.

"You can do *anything*, Odge Gribble. You've just gotten older and you've forgotten, that's all."

"You make an excellent point . . . for a human," Magdelena said, appearing through the wall.

"What have you got against humans?" Lina whispered. "You live with lots of them, all coming and going at your hotel."

Magdelena shrugged. "They're always screaming at me. I'm not even that scary; I'm just a ghost rat—"

"Did you hear that?" Odge interrupted, crawling over to the window.

Lina hadn't heard a thing. She settled Ray down in the backpack and lifted her head as Odge turned, a look of panic in her eyes, and mouthed, "*RUN!*"

CHAPTER ELEVEN

THE PRISONERS

U P HIGH in the mountains of Mist, the harpies had converted the attic room of Mrs. Smith's troll mansion into a prison cell. They had expected to evict everyone, but with Odge on the loose, Mrs. Smith decided it was best to keep the hag's friends locked up, in case Odge managed to outsmart them and they needed to bargain with her. Despite being a little on the irrational side, Mrs. Smith was wise enough not to underestimate Odge Gribble.

Mrs. Smith was happy to host them. She had the tallest towers, for starters, so there was definitely no way of escaping that didn't involve death. Where once trolls had curled up reading their magazines or gazing at the stars, Netty and Ben now sat huddled together in a cold clump.

"Odge and Lina will find us," Ben said, patting a terrified Netty's back.

She was hyperventilating—not for the reasons he suspected, but because she was locked in a room with *Ben*.

As the most glamorous, gorgeous, boily hag on the Island, she could have her pick of suitors, but it was always Ben who had intrigued her. He was so nice and kind. And, *yes*, he had his downsides—he had no boils, not a single one. And his ear hair was lacking! But there was something magical about him nonetheless.

Netty turned to him and grinned with as many teeth showing as physically possible. Ben held on to his eyebrows.

"Odge will come and save us," Ben said. "I hope she's not throwing a tantrum and complaining about everything being impossible."

He was used to Odge's ways—her mood could change like the weather, and she was wonderfully stubborn.

"Oh, I'm such a beautiful idiot," Netty said. "If I hadn't been so stupid and led the harpies to your hiding place, we wouldn't be in this mess. What if Odge gives up? It'll be all my fault."

"She won't give up," Ben assured her. "She never

gives up. And I don't think Lina will let her."

"You're right! Plus Odge isn't the only hag with plans that could save you—I mean us," Netty said with a wink.

"Is this the hair—"

"The hair-rollers thing? Yes," Netty finished.

"What exactly is the hair-rollers thing?" Ben dared to ask. "Odge said you had a plan that involved them."

"It's better if I don't say," Netty said quietly. "In case they torture you for information."

"About hair rollers?" Ben said, but Netty just winked again.

Ben got to his feet. "Do you think there is a way out? Maybe we could escape?"

"Nope—absolutely no escape," Netty assured him. "I cleaned this room, and the only way out is through that locked door."

Ben peeked through the keyhole and spotted a harpy talon in it.

"Great," he said, sliding down the door. "The gump closes in twenty-four hours, and my parents and all our magical friends will be locked out forever."

"Not forever," Netty said. "Just nine years, until the gump opens again."

"Nine years is too long," Ben said sadly. "And imagine, Netty—nine years locked up in here alone with me."

Netty tried desperately to rearrange her face into an expression that was not one of joy.

CHAPTER TWELVE

TREVOR

LINA AND Odge crawled fast through the streets of Swampton, pursued by the army of swamp fairies that had returned for the night after evicting most of the rebellion. The rest could wait on boats until the morning.

"I can't believe they're back already," Odge hissed. "I thought we would have time to sleep!"

"And make a plan to defeat the harpies!" Lina added.

Unlike harpies, who shrieked and cackled, swamp fairies were deadly quiet. It was only the smell that gave them away. Most people, when they get a whiff of sewage, imagine it to be a burst pipe or an off sandwich—but on Mist it is almost always something much more sinister.

Lina pinched her nose as Odge pushed her fast through a town square, complete with a little gloopy fountain and bewildered-looking frogs.

"*There!*" came an ear-piercing voice. "I see them!"

Lina turned to see a small clump of swamp fairies hurtling toward them. Odge grabbed her hand, and they shot off through the maze of gloopy streets, the clump of fairies growing larger and larger behind them.

"We need to get out of here!" Odge shouted. "I bet, if we can just climb the buildings, we can break through the magical layer of swamp water."

"But they'll see you leave," said Magdelena, who was scuttling along beside them.

"If we can get up there without them seeing, the swamp water is so thick that they won't see us swimming about up there," Lina said, talking fast. "They'll spend hours searching Swampton, not knowing we've already left!"

Ray jiggled about in Lina's backpack as they charged through the streets.

"But there's no way we can climb the tiny buildings, Lina!" Odge said. "In case you haven't noticed, in Swampton, we are quite massive. They'll see us."

Lina swung her backpack and unzipped it. She'd had an idea.

"Ray," Lina whispered. "I know you probably can't make mist, just like the other mistmakers on the Island, but we really need to lose the fairies and get out of this swamp. If there is any way you can, please will you make some?"

"They have nowhere to go!" a swamp fairy squealed in delight. "Nowhere at all!"

It was then that the most remarkable thing happened—Ray opened his mouth, sending a perfect stream of mist sailing through the air. It mingled with the clump of swamp fairies until they were more of a fluffy cloud than a smelly swarm.

Odge leaped up onto one of the buildings and pulled Lina up too.

"I'll go and create noise in a building over there to distract them," Magdelena said with a wink, and then she disappeared.

Odge and Lina stood tall on the building while the swamp fairies screamed and tried to fight through the mist. On her tiptoes, Lina could break through the magical layer of the swamp and poke her head out. It was so serene up there—all steamy, warm, and filled with birdsong.

"The bank of the swamp is just ahead," Odge said, winking gloop out of her eye. "Come on."

Lina watched as Odge leaped onto the bank, landing in the soft mud. She followed, landing just short of it, and had to swim fast to the edge.

Lina hastily got to her feet. "Now what?" she asked, just as she and Odge began to sink.

Odge scowled. "Those flying pests—they're quick-mudding us."

Lina could feel herself sinking through the mud, and with every move she made it just digested her some more. She stayed still, not moving a muscle.

Odge rolled her eyes. "It's at times like this that I wish I were one of the more magical ones. A quick spell would sort this right out. Best thing I can do is grow impressive armpit hair. And often, I can't even do that!"

"Not the time!" Lina shouted as some reeds snapped onto her wrists, and Odge's too, and the pair of them were pulled clean out of the mud and hoisted into a tree.

At the top, holding the reeds, was an impossibly small swamp fairy, who introduced himself as Trevor. He was a squat little thing with a musty smell and a hat made of stacked lily pads.

"You'll be safe here," he whispered.

"Um, aren't you . . ." Lina paused, unsure whether to say it. "On *their side*?"

Trevor grinned. "It wasn't for me. I don't like what the harpies have done to this island. I'm also a *huge* Ben and royal-family fan. They say you're leading the rebellion and are going to help us all," he said, brushing the gloop off Odge's blue boots.

"I probably won't help your *friends*," Odge replied, to the sounds of "FIND 'EM AND KILL 'EM!" below. "They aren't the nicest creatures, are they?"

"Some of them aren't so bad," Trevor said. "I think they're just afraid of being hunted by the harpies or thrown out themselves if they don't do what they're told."

"Pah!" Odge said. "That's no excuse. Imagine if they all decided not to fight for the harpies—they'd be without an army and much easier to stop. Not standing up for what is right is the *worst* kind of bad, if you ask me."

Trevor bowed his head, but said nothing. There wasn't anything to say.

"You'll stay here until light, and then I will come and collect you. The tree is safe and magic." He snapped a branch, making it sprout more leaves to completely conceal them. "They won't look for you here—the trees are too tall. They'd never imagine you could get to the top without magic. Now I must go back to Swampton and pretend I'm one of them."

He waved and whispered, "Ben forever!" before flying off, taking his distinctly musty smell with him.

Lina lifted a leaf and peeked out. The fairies were walking two to a row up and down and around the swamp, searching every inch of it.

"It's actually quite fun to watch them, isn't it?" Odge said with a satisfied smirk. "Look at them searching in completely the wrong place."

Lina looked around the tree. The branches curled up and around each other, creating a cozy, leaf-lined room. "I'm so glad Trevor exists. We would've never got up here without his magic. We would need to fly to get so high!"

"That's the problem with these swamp fairies and harpies," Odge groaned. "The flying—they're impossible to stop when in the air."

"What if Mrs. Smith weren't airborne?" Lina asked, an idea coming to her.

Odge shook her head. "Flying high is what she does—if she sees you, the first thing she does is rise up and fly around. And you can't defeat her that way. You saw them in action."

Lina lay on her back and sighed, dangling her arms at her sides. She felt like she had the answer right there, but just an inch out of reach. She thought of meeting Odge and their journey here. Her stomach rumbled at the memory of the delicious chocolate torte. She snapped back up, her eyes wide. "Odge," she said urgently. "*Odge?*"

"Yes?" Odge said, not taking her eyes off the swamp fairies.

"At the hotel, when we were eating torte, before Ray got huge, you told me about your aunt in London. Do you remember?"

"Yes," Odge said absently. "She's the only one in my family who lives in the human world."

"But you said something else—you said she was excellent at something."

Odge looked up and whipped round to face Lina. "Balding people!" she cried, covering her mouth when she realized how loudly she'd said it.

Lina nodded, a huge grin spreading across her face. "*Balding.* If we can get your aunt to bald the harpies, they won't have feathers to fly. Then we'd have a chance against them."

"Lina, you're a genius! But you know what this means, don't you?"

Lina nodded excitedly.

"We need to take a trip to London," Odge said, smiling as the memories flooded back. "We need to go to Platform Thirteen."

CHAPTER THIRTEEN

PLATFORM THIRTEEN

LINA BARELY slept that night, in part because she was balancing on a branch in a tree (in the smelliest swamp imaginable), but also because she was excited to visit London with Odge.

Trevor had arrived at dawn and, as promised, helped them out of the tree and back to the cove. From there, they stowed away on the last of the boats taking the rebels across the lake to the gump and arrived at the cave where a harpy hovered, eagerly kicking creatures from the rebellion out one by one.

"Beasts," the harpy guarding the gump sneered.

"Odge, what if they recognize us?" Lina whispered.

Odge's eyes grew wide. "Oh no, I didn't think of that. I am *very* well known among the harpies, as you can imagine."

"Excuse me, but could you do us a huge favor?" Lina said, turning to a troll and tugging on her beard. "We need to get through unnoticed, and I was wondering if we could hide behind your impressive beard?"

The troll looked delighted at the compliment and lifted her beard, and her friend did the same for Odge.

"Good thinking, Lina," Odge whispered, from somewhere under fifty years' worth of hair growth.

"Beasts, yuck, ugh, beasts," the harpy snapped, occasionally kicking a magical creature for effect.

Lina could feel Ray shaking in her backpack, but there was no need to be worried. The troll beards worked a treat, and soon they were walking through the long tunnel toward Platform Thirteen.

The smell of salty seas was soon overpowered by the smell of sweet soaps and sandwiches, coffee and croissants. The rumble of trollies and trains filled the tunnel, and soon Lina could see people on distant platformsreal human people— running to catch their trains. Odge linked arms with Lina as they stepped into the bright light of King's Cross Station.

Odge stopped to take it all in, her eyes glistening with tears.

"Are you all right?" Lina asked.

Odge smiled at the platform as if it were a long-lost friend. "I'm more than all right."

A ghost dressed in a porter's uniform was hovering there to meet everyone, directing the poor bewildered magical creatures to places where they could stay. "The witches have rooms on Portland Place and Northcote Road," he said, tipping his cap.

Odge stared at him, mouth ajar.

"What is it?" Lina asked, prodding her. "You look like you've seen a ghost! Well, I suppose he is a ghost, but still . . . Haven't you seen a ghost before?"

Odge had seen a ghost before, of course, and Lina knew that. What she didn't know was that Odge had seen this particular ghost before, when she first came to Platform Thirteen all those years ago. But Ernie Hobbs, despite being very old and very dead, now looked very different. His thin frame was now fleshed out, and the buttons on his shirt were bursting.

"Is that our Odge?" he asked in amazement,

turning his attention to the two girls. "And . . . Ben?" he guessed, looking at Lina.

"It is me!" Odge said, wrapping her arms through the ghost. "And of course that's not Ben, Mr. Hobbs."

"Yes," Mr. Hobbs said. "You're quite right."

"This is my friend Lina," Odge said. "Lina, this is Ernie Hobbs."

"A pleasure," Lina said, curtsying, which made Ernie Hobbs laugh and tip his cap.

"He's put on weight, hasn't he?" came another voice.

Lina watched as another ghost, with long gray hair and sparkling eyes, glided into view.

"Oh, hello, Mrs. Partridge! I did think he looked a little different," Odge said, as the ghost floated down to a bench and crossed her legs.

"We decided to swap, you see," Mrs. Partridge said. "Our jobs, I mean. I was the cleaner, and Ernie was the railway porter, and we had done it for years. So one day we thought we'd have a change. Well, of course Ernie took over my cleaning duties right around the time they were doing up the station. Odge, you'll notice it is quite changed, though luckily we managed to keep them off Platform Thirteen. But they added more food shops than I can count, and we all know what happens when food goes off."

"It becomes ghost food," Odge explained to Lina.

"I really like cleaning," Ernie said as an old baguette floated up and straight into his mouth.

Mrs. Partridge rolled her eyes. "I am very much enjoying my new role as railway porter."

"And I am *so enjoying* being the cleaner," Ernie said, catching three ghost muffins as they sailed past. "Someone's got to do it!"

"Off to look for my umbrella," a ghostly woman informed them as she sailed fast toward the Lost Luggage Office.

Lina could tell why this was Odge's favorite gump—there was something so homey about it, despite it being filled with ghosts. It wasn't as fancy as the one in Vienna; in fact, it was quite shabby. But the warm glow of sunlight on bricks and the funny duo that was Ernie and Mrs. Partridge made Lina forget about the harpies for a moment. She imagined what it must've been like for Odge, arriving at Platform Thirteen when she was her age. Her first time in the human world!

"We're here to find my aunt Maureen," Odge said. "And we don't have much time."

"Ah," Ernie said. "Balding Maureen. I'll get you some pennies from the lost-property tin— London is expensive these days."

"She won't be easy to find, I fear," Mrs. Partridge said. "Ever since the harpies' takeover and rumors that you were leading the rebellion reached us—well done, by the way!—she's been moving from place to place. She's worried the harpies may come for her. Use her as bait as a way to get to you."

"What was her last known address?" Lina asked. "We could start there."

"No," Odge said. "When someone is lost, we always start with the pearly mermaids."

Mrs. Partridge nodded in approval.

"Who," Lina asked, "are the *pearly mermaids*?"

CHAPTER FOURTEEN

THE TUBE

LINA HAD only ever read about the London Underground in books; she'd never actually seen it.

They'd boarded a tube from King's Cross and were going around London on the Circle Line, but to where, exactly, Lina wasn't sure, and she certainly wasn't about to start quizzing Odge about it in front of the humans.

She hugged her backpack tightly, giving it a pat every so often to reassure Ray that she was still there and everything was absolutely fine.

Everyone in their carriage looked so dazed and bored that she wondered if they had been sitting in their seats for years. A young woman across from her was blowing bright pink gum bubbles, her arm flopped across the empty seat next to her.

But it wasn't empty for long—a small ghost

boy in a blazer and school cap got on at the next stop and plonked himself down in the seat to the left of the woman with the bubblegum. His scratchy-looking knitted socks struggled to cling to his legs, and he was muddy, as if he'd been wading through rubble all day. He stared around the carriage sadly as if he were used to being ignored, but his face brightened when his eyes fell on Lina.

"Hello," he said, tipping his cap. "Where are you from?"

"She's from Vienna," Odge replied, before picking up a newspaper and burying her nose in it.

The young woman with the chewing gum nodded in awkward acknowledgment, mistakenly assuming, it appeared, that Odge's comment was directed at her.

"Can no one else see him?" Lina whispered to Odge.

The boy beamed at Lina.

"You have to believe in them first," Odge muttered as the Tube ground to a halt. She threw down her newspaper. "This is our stop. Good-bye, you cheeky mud-covered little ghost boy!"

The young woman with the chewing gum looked offended.

Lina waved good-bye to the boy and trotted

after Odge. She was difficult to keep up with sometimes, walking in bounding strides that forced Lina to break into a jog.

They'd alighted at a station Lina had never heard of before: Blackfriars. She knew all the usual ones—Oxford Circus, Piccadilly Circus, Baker Street, Paddington, but not this one.

"We just need to find Temperance. She'll be around here somewhere," Odge said, raising a hand to her head like a pirate and scanning the street.

"What does she look like?" Lina asked.

"Um, well, I've never actually met her, but she's got a Grecian dress on, her hair is pulled back, and she's holding a jug."

"Right," Lina said slowly, wondering if Odge had perhaps got that wrong. Then again, if she was right, Temperance was going to be very easy to find.

"Ah," Odge said, pointing to someone up ahead, "there she is!"

The person Odge was pointing at was a middle-aged man yelling into his telephone. "Odge, I don't think that could possibly be—"

"Behind him," Odge said, walking fast in the direction in which she'd pointed.

Lina followed, and they came to a stop, just

past the angry man, at a statue of a woman perched atop a fountain.

"Temperance is a statue?" Lina asked. She supposed that did make more sense than a real lady in a Grecian dress walking around London with a jug.

"We'll wait until he leaves," Odge said, nodding at the man on the phone, who had now turned a furious shade of purple. "Don't want him to see anything."

They waited patiently while the man screamed words like *"CUSTOMER SERVICE"* and *"LAWSUIT"* before accepting something for free, and then he was off.

They both turned and looked up at the statue. She was beautiful, with a long mane of neatly tamed hair. In her hand was a jug, tipped forward, spilling out imaginary water. A pathetic dribble of real water snaked out from under one of her toes instead.

Odge spotted Lina's unimpressed expression. "They couldn't make it an impressive fountain or else it would attract the crowds." She cracked her knuckles. "Right, let's try this. My mother once told me about a holiday she took to see the pearly mermaids, and I've never forgotten the password." She turned her attention to the statue. "Hello there, Temperance. I like your plates of meat."

"WHAT?" Lina cried. "She's got a jug, not plates of meat."

Odge shot her an irritated look, but her face quickly softened. "Ah, of course. You're Viennese, so you probably don't know Cockney rhyming slang. *Plates of meat* means *feet*."

As soon as Odge finished, water began to gush from the jug.

"Quickly," she said, "hold your hand in it."

Lina obliged, though she didn't want to. The water was filthy and as thick as gravy. She indulged Odge, holding her hand still, palm up. And then it happened—a small, perfect pearl landed in her hand. She closed her fingers around it so it didn't wash away.

"Did you get one?" Odge asked hopefully, holding up a pearl.

Lina nodded and gripped it tighter. "Now what?"

"Thanks, Temperance!" Odge said, looking around. "There should be stairs that lead us down under the bridge. Ah—there they are!"

The steps lay barely a few skips from where

Temperance stood, and within seconds they were standing hidden under the bridge arches.

The pearly mermaids lived in a very old and secret part of London known as the River Fleet. It ran from the ponds of Hampstead all the way down to where they were standing at Black-friars Bridge. In Victorian times, the humans had decided that the river, which they barely used at all, should be incorporated into the sewage system. "You can imagine how annoyed the pearly mermaids were about *that*," Odge said.

"They live in a sewer?" Lina said with a shudder.

Odge smiled. "But I've heard they've done wonders with the place!" She leaned over the edge and tossed her pearl into the water.

Lina followed suit, but she was surprised by the sound it made—it didn't make a *plop* as she'd expected, but rather hit the water with an almighty *crack*, like a firework exploding under the surface.

At first nothing happened, and Lina wondered if perhaps Odge had misremembered, and they'd wasted their only chance. Would Temperance give them another pearl, or was that it? But to her relief the water began to bubble, slowly at first, and then more aggressively. Glints of silver and gold flashed under the surface, like treasure ready to be found.

"Stand back," Odge said, pulling Lina by the backpack as the water began to spit at them. The clanking groans of long-forgotten metal echoed around them, and then out of the water burst two lopsided spiral staircases, covered excessively in pearls of every size.

There was no time to waste. Lina jumped onto the staircase and tried to steady her feet as they began their descent. A thin layer of gunk covered each step, making it a slow process. Lina looked up, wondering if any of the humans walking the bridge might think to peer over and catch a glimpse of them.

She stopped when she was neck-deep in water and looked around, expecting to see a secret passageway like the gump on Platform Thirteen, but there was nothing—just more water and bridge stumps.

"We have to keep going a little farther," Odge explained. "You can hold your breath."

"What about Ray?" Lina cried.

"He's a mistmaker," Odge said. "They're amphibians. It'll only be for two minutes or so."

"TWO MINUTES?"

Two minutes was a ridiculously long time. She

had *asthma*. She was about to say so when Odge leaned over and squeezed her hand.

"Just follow the staircase, and you can't go wrong." And then she disappeared under the water.

"Odge!" Lina cried, dunking her head under. "Odge!" She came back up, spitting grimy water. The spiral staircases creaked and swayed, shifting slightly in the tide.

Lina imagined what her birthday would've been like if she'd chosen the long weekend in Salzburg. She would've avoided a swamp chase, a harpy talon to the head, and now potentially dying on a pearly staircase under a bridge she had never heard of before.

She closed her eyes. She was here now, so she might as well finish this. It was her mission, after all, and she had convinced Odge there was hope.

She took a deep breath and went under, pulling herself down the staircase. At one point, she lost her grip, and her legs floated up above her, disorientating her completely. She kept on, her hands shaking as she held tight to the pearly banister. Finally she reached the bottom, but when she did there was nothing—no Odge, no pearly mermaids (whatever they were), and no visibility. The water was gravy-thick.

The staircase groaned and began to retract, folding itself back into the watery depths from where it had come. Lina's mind raced: maybe the pearly mermaids weren't letting her in because she was a human; maybe she'd done something wrong; maybe this was it.

She turned to swim to the surface, but something pulled her back. It glinted in front of her—a string of pearls in the near darkness. She grabbed hold of it, unsure if it was a good idea or not, and swam down, following the string until she reached a narrow tunnel. Through she went, kicking her legs as fast as she could, willing herself to hold her breath for a few more seconds. Up ahead, she could see bright light and the silhouettes of people on the surface. Huge hats of feathers and pearls and a hag that looked awfully familiar.

"You did it!" Odge cheered, fishing Lina from the water and setting her down in a puddle.

Lina gulped in air and rubbed her eyes, her hands still shaking. Hushed whispers and the *plops* of a million droplets of water filled her ears. They were in a grand old tunnel, lined with a knee-deep stream of sewage water and peppered with garlands of pearls. And all around, in every corner, crevice, and pool of water, lounged the pearly mermaids.

"You brought a human with you, hag?" a mermaid said, staring intently at Lina. "You know we 'ave a no-human rule."

"She's not one of *those* humans," Odge countered.

The mermaid looked about twelve years old. He had long dark hair and a pearly waistcoat. His tail scales were colored a sewage brown with a pearlescent sheen.

Another young mermaid popped out from the stream of water. She was about Lina's age and had bright green eyes. She wore a crown of pearls and soaked feathers. "Where you from?"

"Vienna," Lina said quietly, feeling a little shy.

"I ain't never heard of that one," the mermaid said, pulling herself out of the water. "I'm Cholly. This is my big brother, Plomtee."

"I once knew a mermaid called Plomlee," Odge said. "She lived in the Pimlico swimming baths and had a terrible singing voice because of the chlorine."

"That's our mam," Cholly said. "We grew up in those swimming baths. Then she decided to move back home, and 'ere we are."

"Is she here?" Odge asked. "It would be nice to see her again."

"She's up Hampstead Ponds 'avin' lunch wiv her friends. But what can we 'elp you wif?"

All the pearly mermaids edged closer, apparently very keen to see why this fantastical hag and human girl had come so far to see them.

"We need help locating Odge's aunt," Lina explained. "Her aunt Maureen."

"Baldin' Maureen!" Plomtee cheered. "Yeah, we know 'er. We have a right bubble bath wi' her."

"*Bubble bath* is cockney rhyming slang for *laugh*," Odge whispered to Lina.

"You want us to locate 'er, then?" Cholly asked. "We can do that, for a small fee."

"We don't have anything to pay you with," Lina said. "We used the only change we found to buy tickets for the Tube."

"What's in that backpack you got?" Plomtee asked.

"A mistmaker," Odge said, before Lina could stop her.

The pearly mermaids began to whisper excitedly.

"We could use one of them down 'ere, we could," Cholly said.

"He's not for sale," Lina said quickly. "He's a beloved pet."

Cholly and Plomtee exchanged looks.

Odge smiled at Lina. "Yes, he belongs to the Prince. We cannot trade him, I'm afraid; it wouldn't be proper."

If there was one thing pearly mermaids respected, it was royalty. They had their own royals and were big fans of the royal family of Mist, even if they *were* human.

"Anything else," Lina said. "Just not Ray."

Cholly's eyes shifted from Lina to Odge's feet. "I could do with 'aving a pair of them blue boots."

"But you don't even have plates of meat!" Lina said, making the entire underground tunnel of pearly mermaids erupt into hysterical laughter.

"She's getting the 'ang of 'ow we speak down 'ere, in't she, Odge?"

Odge laughed too, although Lina noticed she had shifted her feet so one boot toe was sitting protectively over the other.

"Fine," Odge said eventually, reluctantly taking the boots off. "The boots for the location of Aunt Maureen."

Cholly reached out her hands, eagerly grabbing for them. Her tail flopped about behind her, splashing water up onto the crumbling ceiling bricks.

"But they're your favorite thing," Lina whispered.

Odge handed them over. "No. My friends are my favorite thing—and if this can save them, then I don't need my blue boots."

"We've got a replacement for you!" came a shout from a mermaid farther down the tunnel. A pair of tattered old leather boots came soaring through the air and landed at Odge's feet. They were soggy, and the heels were missing. "From the late seventeenth century, those—proper antique."

Odge managed to force a "thank you" before pulling them on. She stepped to the side, making a squelching noise.

"You suit 'em!" Cholly said. "Now Plomtee will find your aunt."

"How long will it take?" Lina asked.

Cholly stroked her chin for a moment, apparently really considering the question. "Could take five minutes; could take five days."

"Five days?" Lina cried. "We don't have that much time. The gump will close tonight at nine o'clock. We only have hours, not days."

Plomtee dived into the water and swam off.

"Well then, you better hope it takes hours," Cholly said.

Lina sat back down on the cold stone floor and stared off into the dark tunnel, exhausted and feeling helpless for the first time. All they could do was wait.

"Look at them mince pies," Cholly said, pointing at Lina's face. "They got fear in 'em."

"*Mince pies* means *eyes*," Odge whispered.

CHAPTER FIFTEEN

THE ROBBERS

THE HARPIES flew so fast through the gump that Ernie Hobbs mistook them for out-of-date turkeys and would've tried to eat them were it not for Mrs. Partridge pulling him back so they could slide through the wall and hide. The last thing the ghosts wanted was an encounter with Mrs. Smith.

Unfortunately, being in a wall, the ghostly pair didn't see where it was the harpies were going, and of course they instantly worried about Lina and Odge. And they were right to be worried, because that's exactly why the harpies had come to London. The rock monsters had been gossiping again and had revealed that the human girl and Odge Gribble had made their way through the gump with the last of the rebels. While all the others believed Odge had given up, Mrs. Smith knew better. Believing Odge was headed to London to recruit enough magical creatures to storm back through the gump, she had decided it was time to stop Odge's meddling, once and for all.

The harpies stuck to the roof of King's Cross Station, briefly flying outside before swooping into another part of the building that had a sign above it reading ST. PANCRAS INTERNATIONAL.

Mrs. Smith, Miss Witherspoon, Miss Green, and Miss Brown all bowed their heads in respect, mistaking the sign to be a tribute to Saint Pancreas, the international saint of eating pancreases and other body parts—a harpy favorite.

Below the arched glass ceiling, baked goods, chocolates, and colorful sweets spilled across tables in shops like delicious jewels. There were clothes shops and gift shops and, in the middle of it all, a woman screamed.

"IT STOLE MY COAT!" she cried over and over again. "THE BIG BIRD WITH THE HUMAN FACE STOLE MY COAT!"

It wasn't long before a shop worker telephoned the police, mistaking her for a madwoman. That's the problem when a harpy steals your coat—there is absolutely no way of informing people without them deeming you insane.

Mrs. Smith had plumped for the woman in the fancy coat, leaving the other three to steal the raincoats from three men, who were instantly taken more seriously when they shouted about half-birds with human faces.

Talons can make quick work of unraveling a human from their coat, and so the harpies were at the other end of the station before the humans realized they were gone. No one stopped to question why the woman in the expensive coat was walking so strangely—with an impossible curve of the spine as if she were nothing but a head, neck, and sack of flesh wobbling under a coat.

They stumbled into a coffee shop and waited in line. They had no intention of getting coffee. When they got to the front of the queue, Mrs. Smith barked, "HAVE YOU SEEN A HAG AND A LITTLE GIRL?"

The man almost laughed, which was a mistake. Mrs. Smith had no time for jokers. She poked a talon out of the coat, startling the man.

"A *HAG*," she repeated again, slowly so he could understand. "AND A *GIRL*."

"With all due respect, so many people pass through this station every day. I can only tell you for certain, I have never seen a hag."

Mrs. Smith narrowed her eyes. "She looks

quite human. Blue boots. She arrived at Platform Thirteen at King's Cross."

"This is a different station," the man explained. "And I don't think anyone uses Platform Thirteen these days—do they, Kevin?" He turned to look at his colleague, but when he looked back, the strange old woman had gone.

Ernie Hobbs and Mrs. Partridge were discussing the harpies back on Platform Thirteen.

"No, Ernie—Miss Jones *wasn't* with them just now," Mrs. Partridge insisted. "She's the one with the big hats, remember? The harpy who, last time the gump opened, asked to borrow some suitcases for little furry pets she had or something like that. She'd got the idea from somewhere that they liked sleeping in them—you remember her!"

"Was she the one who smelled of rotten intestines?"

Mrs. Partridge tutted. "They *all do*, Ernie."

Ernie was about to ask Mrs. Partridge what she thought the harpies were doing in London when Mrs. Smith landed with a thud in front of them.

"Where's Odge and the human girl?" she seethed.

Ernie Hobbs was no good at lying, and so Mrs.

Partridge had given him one of her looks. He knew it meant, *Say nothing, or there will be hell to pay.*

"We haven't seen them," Mrs. Partridge said firmly. Being dead already, she wasn't afraid of Mrs. Smith.

Mrs. Smith swayed in her coat, turning so red and getting so furious she could barely spit the words out.

"Oh, actually," Ernie Hobbs said, making Mrs. Partridge visibly wince, "I do remember where they went, Mrs. Smith."

"Where?" she demanded, curling a talon under his squidgy ghost chin. Even though he knew it couldn't hurt him, he recoiled.

"Borough Market," he said joyfully, the thrill of deceiving them all too obvious in his voice. "THEY WENT TO BOROUGH MARKET!"

"I'll get you a cab," Mrs. Partridge said with a smirk.

And so the ghosts got back to work, delighted the harpies had been distracted and deceived. The only problem was that Plomtee was swimming his way back to Lina and Odge with a location for Aunt Maureen, and though Ernie Hobbs couldn't have possibly known it, he had just made a terrible, terrible mistake.

CHAPTER SIXTEEN

THE PIGEONS

PLOMTEE DIDN'T take five days to locate Aunt Maureen—he took a mere fifty minutes, which was incredibly impressive. When he arrived back at the Blackfriars base, he found Odge and Lina asleep, using Cholly's tail as a pillow.

"Should I wake 'em?" Cholly whispered.

Plomtee raised himself up on his elbows and peeked over at them. "They did say they ain't got much time, Cholly."

Cholly wriggled her tail, and Lina awoke with a snort.

"Found 'er," Plomtee said proudly. "She was chattin' to 'erself inside the cat and dog down Borough Market."

Lina rubbed her eyes, unsure if she was still asleep—how could someone be *inside* a cat *and* a dog. Really, they couldn't be inside either, but definitely not both.

"*Cat and dog* means *bog*," Odge whispered. "And *bog* means *toilet*."

"So we need to go to Borough Market," Lina said. "Is it far?"

Cholly smiled. "I'll get you a cab."

The cab was an old battered boat smothered in pearls and shimmering buttons. Two old mermaids pulled it out from the safety of the secret underground lair and along the River Thames. Luckily, the people on the shores were too busy trying to get to where they were going or admiring London's glinting architectural delights to notice the little boat. Nevertheless, Odge and Lina still ducked. They pulled up on Bankside, a little east of Southwark Bridge, and dismounted, saying good-bye to the pearly mermaids. Cholly had swum alongside the boat, eager to see her new friends to their destination.

"I hope you find Baldin' Maureen an' she 'elps you with them horrible harpies," she said. "And if you get kicked out of Mist you can live wiv us. You too, Vienna." She waved good-bye and dived under the water.

"Take the apples and pears there to the frog and toad," one of the pearly mermaids pulling the boat said.

"*Apples and pears* means *stairs*, and *frog and toad* means *road*," Odge translated as they watched the mermaids, and the entire boat, disappear underwater.

It was only a short walk to the market, and when they arrived, Lina felt a renewed sense of hope that they'd be able to make everything right. They were getting somewhere—if they could locate Aunt Maureen and convince her to come to Mist, they could stop the harpies, return the evicted magical creatures, and save the mistmakers before the gump closed! She was delighted, and she was also starving, so she made a beeline for the bakery with its rainbow cakes and swirly chocolate buns showing off their deliciousness in the window.

Odge grabbed Lina's arm. When Lina turned, she was surprised to see Odge's face frozen in shock.

"Odge?" she whispered. "What's wrong?" Somewhere, deep down, she knew, but she didn't want to believe it.

Odge pointed at the crowds milling around the fruit stalls. "There."

Lina looked over and couldn't see anything

out of the ordinary, but then the woman in the expensive coat turned round.

Lina began to shake. Slowly, the pair of them stepped backward. Lina wished the bakery would gobble them up and spit them out somewhere else.

Mrs. Smith's eyes fell upon them, and she grinned.

"Run!" Odge cried.

Mrs. Smith and the others began to run, wobbling frantically as they went.

"How rude!" a man cried as they pushed him out of the way.

"Excuse you!" another shouted as Mrs. Smith pushed a child into a pile of watermelons.

Lina ran fast past a cheese shop that reminded her of Hans and down a quiet cobbled street.

Odge stopped beside her and doubled over, trying to catch her breath. "How did they find us?"

Lina pulled Odge to the side, and the pair of them ducked behind a large bin. It smelled of the swamp fairies, and Lina had an urge to run, but she reminded herself it was just a bin. It may have smelled like them, but it was *just* rubbish.

"We wait here," Lina whispered. "Wait until they go, and then we'll find your aunt."

"They won't go," Odge whispered back. "We have to get rid of them."

Lina could hear the *click-clack* of talons on cobblestones. She held her breath. Odge fiddled with the bin. It was a large dumpster-style one on wheels. She rolled it back and forth, inspecting it.

"What are you doing?" Lina hissed as the thing squeaked. "They'll hear us."

"How heavy do you think this bin is?" Odge said, not even attempting to lower her voice.

The *click-clacking* stopped.

Lina looked up, convinced they'd been heard. She could feel her heart pounding in her mouth. A tall shadow appeared at the end of the alleyway, stretching up the wall until it hovered sinisterly above them.

"I know you're there, Odge and human girl," Mrs. Smith snapped. "Remember we have Ben and Netty, so don't do anything silly."

"I WOULD NEVER!" Odge said, leaping up and shoving the bin.

It careered fast down the alleyway, knocking into cobblestones and flying sideways. Mrs. Smith, in a fluster, began madly shouting directions to the harpies, but it just caused confusion, until half went one way and half went another.

Mrs. Smith looked back just in time to see the bin make contact with her face. She was whipped backward before bursting from her coat in a rage and taking flight.

Odge and Lina charged out of the alleyway back toward Borough Market. Odge grabbed the coat and threw it to Lina.

"What now?" Lina shouted, putting the coat on. It seemed the most sensible and efficient way of carrying it.

"I don't know!" Odge said. "We'll figure it out. They can hardly attack us in front of humans. The last thing they'd want would be to be seen by lots of witnesses—people might start asking questions, and then who knows—their beloved island might be discovered and known by all humans, like it once was. No, they wouldn't want that—they'd fear an invasion!"

"I don't think they're going to give up without a fight," Lina said, gasping for breath. A stitch nipped at her side, and the expensive coat was weighing her down.

They arrived back in the market and weaved through the stalls, looking out for the harpies and Aunt Maureen.

Lina crouch-walked past people.

"Can you see them?" Odge whispered.

Lina scanned the market and spotted Miss Witherspoon crouching at the end of the sausage stall to her left. She'd lined her nose up perfectly so it looked like a deflated, spindly piece of meat in the row of juicy sausages.

"I hope someone tries to eat it," Odge spat.

To her right, Lina could see Miss Green and Miss Brown lurking behind barrels of wine. And up above, folded into the rafters with the pigeons, was the tall and gangly Mrs. Smith.

"We're surrounded," Lina whispered. "There's no way out."

Magdelena appeared with a pop. "Well, this is quite the mess, isn't it? Who eats food *from a stall*?"

"Magdelena," Odge whispered urgently. "This is not a good time."

The little ghost rat surveyed the scene, her gaze landing on Mrs. Smith and the others. "I think you need a little help."

"Oh, would you?" Lina said. "I'd be so grateful if you could."

Magdelena scrunched up her face. "Not me, Lina. The pigeons. Ask the pigeons."

"Ask them what?"

"Well, they are big fans of Mist. They're always talking about it, but of course you don't know that because you don't speak pigeon. Pigeons, on the other hand, are much cleverer—they understand pigeon *and* English. Ask them to help you get rid of the harpies. I'm positive they'd be thrilled to help. I'd ask them for you, but I'm a rat—I can't be seen speaking to a *pigeon*."

"But people call pigeons the rats of the sky," Lina pointed out.

"Pah, they should be so lucky!"

Odge was crouched by the fruit stall, her eyes fixed on Mrs. Smith. "She wouldn't dare attack us in a bustling market."

"*Try me,*" Mrs. Smith mouthed, brandishing a talon.

A pigeon toddled up and pecked at Odge's horrible new boots.

"Excuse me," Lina whispered to it. "Could you help us get rid of those harpies? We have important business here in the market, and we need them gone."

The pigeon flew off, making Lina feel incredibly silly. But then the strangest thing happened—the pigeon took a seat next to the others on the rafters and began cooing until every single pigeon in the market was making noise.

People covered their ears as the noise grew louder and louder. And then, like a swarm of feathery bees, the pigeons took off, moving fast toward the harpies, pecking at them one at a time, until all four harpies were lost within a swirling mass of feathers.

"I swear I saw a giant eagle in there! Twice as tall as me!" a woman cried, pointing at the cloud of birds. "It had a ghastly face."

Odge and Lina watched in amazement as the harpies tried to fight their way through the pigeons.

"We could capture them!" Odge shouted, jumping up onto the stall and reaching up high.

"Odge!" Lina cried. "Don't be silly. They may be trapped in a clump of pigeons, but they still have talons, and they're right above your head and wishing you dead!"

Odge climbed down and left the pigeons to it.

"IT *IS* AN EAGLE!" the woman cried again. "DID YOU SEE IT? RIGHT THERE IN THE MIDDLE."

Crowds gathered under the pigeons in such huge numbers that the harpies' goal of capturing Odge and Lina seemed to quickly shift to just getting out of there unseen. They fought their way through the pigeons and shot off, back toward Platform Thirteen.

Lina was sure she heard Mrs. Smith say, "And that is why we don't visit other countries."

She told Odge, who laughed. "Yes, well, she doesn't enjoy a country that isn't her dictatorship. They'll be on their way home, but now they know we're here it's going to be harder to get back through the gump."

"Do you think they'll do something to Ben and Netty?" Lina asked, a shake in her voice as she did so.

"We won't let them," Odge said, wrapping her arm round Lina.

The pigeons settled down, and the humans got back to eating. Lina spotted a stall owner inspecting Mrs. Smith's handbag.

"Oh, look, Odge!" Lina cried, suddenly realizing what a strange name Odge was to a human. "That man has found *your* handbag!"

Odge spun round, and her eyes lit up. "Ah, yes, *my* handbag. I dropped it, see."

The man handed it over with a proud grin. "Nothing gets past me."

Lina smiled, thinking of the four mythical creatures he had failed to see fighting moments ago above his head. Five, if you counted the hag he was speaking to at that very moment.

"Odge, was it?" he asked.

Odge nodded. "Rhymes with *splodge*."

"It's Portuguese," Lina lied. "Very popular name there."

They thanked him again and made their way through the market, swinging the handbag as they went. Lina felt smug in the knowledge that losing it would have annoyed Mrs. Smith.

Odge frowned. "I wonder if that commotion scared my aunt off. If she saw the harpies, she certainly won't be here anymore."

Lina and Odge searched for over an hour—in every shop, down every alleyway, under every stall—and yet they found nothing.

Time was not on their side, and so they found themselves walking the streets that flanked the market, wondering what they should do. They could return to the pearly mermaids and ask them to help again, but that might take hours. They walked past cafés and restaurants and little shops selling newspapers and sweets, and a café full of bald people and a bald cat.

They stopped and turned in unison.

Lina grinned at Odge. "What are the chances of there being a café filled with only bald people and a bald cat?"

CHAPTER SEVENTEEN

THE CAFÉ

AUNT MAUREEN!" Odge cried, flinging the doors open and holding her arms wide.

They still didn't know if she was in there, but Lina could tell Odge was feeling optimistic again. Everyone looked up and stared at them as they walked in.

Odge inspected each table, leaning down and staring closely at each person's face. None of them seemed the slightest bit concerned that they were bald, apart from the cat that was staring wide-eyed at its reflection in the window.

Lina followed behind Odge, holding on tightly to the straps of her backpack and twisting them nervously. If Balding Maureen wasn't in there, all hope would be lost.

An old woman at the back caught her

attention—she was small with normal facial features and a perfectly rounded bald head. She was unremarkable in every way. Just an ordinary human, except for one thing—her eyes were mismatched. One was green, and one was brown.

"Odge?" her aunt said in disbelief.

"Long story," Odge said. "What kind of food do they serve here? We're *starving*."

Lina inhaled a piece of buttery toast while Odge quickly told her aunt about everything.

The café was warm and dimly lit. Little lanterns hung on strings next to dusty Christmas baubles that someone had forgotten to take down. It was quiet, save for the occasional clink of spoons and the murmur of nonmagical conversations. Lina leaned back in her chair and sighed. The café felt like a cocoon, and Aunt Maureen was the glorious bald butterfly buried inside it.

"And then," Odge said, "we got Mrs. Smith's handbag."

Lina shoved the last bit of toast in her mouth and slid the bag across the table.

"I think it's going to have what we need," Odge said excitedly.

Lina shook her head. "No—*you're* what we need, Aunt Maureen."

Aunt Maureen looked from it to Lina and smiled, a naughty glint in her eye. "Well, we should at least open it."

Odge pounded the table with her fist. "*This* is why you're my favorite aunt!"

Odge clicked the clasp and pulled the bag open dramatically.

Almost instantly, everyone in the café got up and charged out the door, including the bald cat.

A putrid purple cloud hung over them.

"Ah," Odge said, "that's the unmistakable stench of Gutsface makeup."

Lina felt as if she were going to faint.

Odge riffled around in the bag, pulling out a little lipstick, which she handed to Lina. It was just a normal lipstick when popped open, only it had a slight curve to navigate the long noses of the harpies.

"Just horrible harpy makeup in here," Odge said. "And a picture of an ogre called Jonathan Whiplet-Warren-Turnip, whose house she stole."

"We need you to help us defeat Mrs. Smith," Lina urged, steering the conversation back to their current crisis, "by balding her so we can catch and overthrow her before the gump closes!"

Aunt Maureen turned to Odge. "You should definitely put Lina on a flight home. She should not be coming back to Mist—many a person has been locked inside or locked out by a gump because of bad timing. You can't predict what will happen!"

Odge turned to Lina and rolled her eyes. "Grown-ups."

"I won't go anywhere from here apart from back through the gump," Lina insisted. "I'm not leaving until I know my friends on Mist are all right."

Aunt Maureen took a sip of her tea, her eyes searching Lina's face. "And you say you need me to bald them?"

Odge and Lina nodded enthusiastically.

"Well, I suppose that can be arranged," she said. "I haven't visited the Island in a long time."

"Why do you live in the human world?" Lina asked.

Aunt Maureen shrugged. "I've always rather liked it. And I look human, so it's easy to move around undetected. Most hags aren't so lucky."

"Most hags are beautiful," Odge said wistfully.

"And, really, this world is as varied as Mist in certain parts. There's nowhere better than London for it, in my opinion."

Lina did love the café—before the Gutsface incident, she'd heard at least four different languages being spoken. Outside, across the street, a Spanish deli dished out tortillas and tapas. And, a little farther along the road, a Japanese restaurant boasted a queue of humans so long and wriggling with excitement that it looked like the restaurant had grown a tail.

Lina agreed—London was magical in its own way, with so many different languages and cultures and cuisines. It was like soaking in all the flavors of the world, all while sitting in the same spot. Vienna was similar—there were amazing friends to meet. What a luxury, she thought, to see so much so easily. She shuddered at the thought of the harpies and how they could tear the magic of a place like London to pieces, like they were doing with Mist.

Odge chewed loudly on the final slice of toast. "Mist has saved many people in its lifetime—it has always been a place of refuge, a place of safety, a place of magic. And I will *never* let the harpies change that."

"Well said, my dear," Aunt Maureen said. "It is our job to make sure as many people feel welcome on Mist as possible, because that is what makes the Island a special place. The problem with creatures like Mrs. Smith is they never have, and never will, understand what real magic is."

Odge gulped down the last bit of toast. "That's why the world needs hags and humans like us."

Lina unzipped her bag to check on Ray. She noticed he was plumper in the human world, and his eyes were less pained. "Time to go back to Mist," she murmured, and she was sure he let out a little whimper. "The harpies will be gone soon," she whispered to him. "I promise."

"Let's go," Odge said, standing up and flinging Mrs. Smith's handbag across the room. It hit the coffee machine and dropped into a bin.

"I'm game," her aunt said. "And I'd like to see that sister of mine while I'm there, after the balding. How is your old mother doing? Still the wartiest?"

Odge's eyes flashed with delight. "No! Netty Pruddle out-warted her!"

Aunt Maureen faux-gasped. "She'll hate that."

CHAPTER EIGHTEEN

THE SCHOOL

THERE WAS a stop they needed to make before returning to Platform Thirteen, and luckily, it was close by.

St. Trilton's School was a squat building nestled between a concrete playground and a concrete car park.

Two hags and a human with a mistmaker hidden in a backpack made their way to the front desks.

"Would it be rude if I held my nose?" Aunt Maureen whispered.

The air in the school was impossibly thick and filled with the smell of school dinners. It was so potent that it seemed as though there should be school dinners smeared on every wall, chair, and child—the fact that the smell came only from the kitchen was quite baffling to Odge.

Lina, on the other hand, was quite used to the smell, though she also found it somewhat overpowering.

"Name?" the receptionist asked.

"The King and Queen of Mist, please," Odge said, forgetting where she was for a second and assuming the woman meant the name of who they were there to visit.

"The . . . *pardon?*"

"We're here to see the lady who deep-fat-fries things and the man who washes the dishes," Lina said.

"Oh, Sue and Sam," the receptionist said. "You're . . . relatives?"

"Obviously not; they're entirely human," Odge said, still forgetting where she was.

The receptionist raised an eyebrow, but didn't say anything. She handed the three of them lanyards to wear round their necks. They had VISITOR stamped on them and also smelled of school dinners.

"Down the hall, third right."

Arriving at a school when an assembly is about to begin and the speaker is running late can cause all sorts of confusion.

"Oh good—you're here," a frazzled teacher said as she caught up with them in the corridor. She ushered a reluctant Odge, Lina, and Aunt Maureen into the big hall. "It's right this way."

The teacher had particularly magnificent curly hair, and Lina could see Aunt Maureen eyeballing it.

Odge obviously noticed too, because she turned to her aunt and said sternly, "*No balding.*"

The crowd of kids sitting neatly with their legs crossed fell silent as the three of them entered the room. Lina tried to turn back, realizing what was happening, but the teacher pushed her on.

"Today, children, we have a very special guest and her . . . friends?" She looked to Odge for an answer.

"She's my friend," Odge said, pointing at Lina. "This is my aunt."

"This is Harriet Rusterfeld, and her friend and aunt, and they have come here today to tell you about what it's like to work as a dentist."

Lina put her head in her hands.

Odge stepped up onto the stage. A kid scowled at her squelchy seventeenth-century boots.

"Sorry about the boots," she whispered. "I had really good ones, and then I had to trade them so some pearly mermaids would go on a sniffer expedition to find my aunt." She gestured to Aunt Maureen. "Found her, though, so it was worth it."

The kids stared up at her. So did the teachers gathered at the back.

Odge smiled at the room. "Well . . . being a dentist, was it? It's very . . . *dentisty* . . ."

Lina shook her head and began pointing at her mouth.

"It's to do with FACES!" Odge cried, as if she were playing charades.

Lina opened her mouth and pointed inside.

"And the inside of mouths? Yeulch."

The kids giggled nervously.

Lina titled her head back, and Aunt Maureen pretended to drill into her teeth.

Odge scrunched up her face. Of all the topics it could have been, dentistry was one of the worst. On Mist, everyone fixed teeth problems with the help of a witch, and they were called Teeth Fixers—or, more officially, the Maggot Teeth Twelve, which didn't sound like "dentist" at all.

"My job as a dentist is to waggle my finger in someone's mouth and—"

Aunt Maureen did a pulling-teeth motion.

"And dance badly, using only my upper body?"

The kids erupted into hysterical laughter, apparently thinking she was joking. It must have been a nice surprise for them—a funny dentist.

"It's a human job—think the Maggot Teeth Twelve," Odge's aunt whispered.

"Ah!" Odge cried, a finger raised in the air. "You learn something new every day!"

She cleared her throat, and the kids fell silent.

"I can tell you *exactly* about my job. I am a dentist, and what dentists do is, when you have a hole in your tooth, or perhaps if one has fallen out completely, we rub a gunk on it and see if it grows back. Sometimes you can pay extra and get an entirely new tooth that's been donated to the Corporation of Tooth Fair—" She stopped, not wanting to say *fairies* in case that blew her cover.

Lina slapped her hand to her head.

"Fair . . . headed dentists," Odge finished.

The schoolteachers were looking at her as if she were mad.

"And that's all there is to it," Odge said, clasping her hands together and bowing. "Oh! And I have a blue molar . . . see!"

The kids began clawing their way to the front to get a better view, tumbling over each other like potatoes rolling out of a bag.

"It's Odge Gribble!" came a cry from the back.

Lina looked up to see a woman with deep-fat-fried hair and a man covered in bubbles.

Odge's jaw hit the floor. "Your Royal Highnesses," she whispered, bowing grandly.

Aunt Maureen did the same.

"And that," Lina cried, "is the end of our show! Comedy with Dentists will be touring the country starting tomorrow. I hope you enjoyed the preview!"

"What on earth is going on?" a teacher hissed. "Sarah, I said a dentist, not a comedy dentist show."

The teacher called Sarah turned beetroot-red, trying to gather the words to explain herself, but she was interrupted by the kids, who got to their feet and clapped loudly.

"Thank you, miss!" they called in unison over to the teacher called Sarah.

"That was much better than we expected!" squeaked a particularly delighted-looking girl at the front.

Lina, Odge, and Aunt Maureen took their chance and ran off to get the King and Queen.

"Pack up your deep-fat fryer and your soap," Odge said with a curtsy. "This is a rescue mission!"

Lina smiled. "We're taking you back to Mist."

CHAPTER NINETEEN

THE BALDING

MRS. SMITH had assigned Miss Witherspoon and Miss Brown the important mission of guarding the gump at Platform Thirteen. If Odge and Lina were going to attempt to return, she was going to make sure there was someone there to stop them. She'd fired the harpy who had been guarding the gump tunnel before, furious that she had let them through in the first place. Of course, that harpy was positive she hadn't seen them—but, then again, she hadn't looked inside the trolls' beards. The old harpy was sent to help shout at the hags doing the troll mansion renovations, and Miss Witherspoon and Miss Brown took her place. Miss Brown guarded the entrance to the gump, and Miss Witherspoon lay in wait in the tunnel.

Ernie Hobbs gobbled down three tuna

baguettes while Miss Brown looked up at him, completely disgusted. He deliberately let out a loud belch because he knew she'd hate it.

Luckily, Lina spotted Miss Brown before they got too close.

"There she is, the harpy—she's waiting for us."

"She looks distracted by Ernie Hobbs's baguette eating," Odge whispered, ducking behind some suitcases. "We just need to get close enough to bald her. The royals will stay here—Aunt Maureen, Lina, and I will go, and we'll let you know when the coast is clear."

The royal pair stood smiling at passing humans who swerved to avoid them. It must have been a strange sight, seeing a man soaked from head to toe and a woman with deep-fried hair standing in the middle of King's Cross Station on a normal afternoon.

Odge led the way, weaving and ducking behind people until they got close to Platform Thirteen. Lina could feel Ray shifting uneasily in her backpack.

"It'll be all right," Lina whispered, reaching a hand back and patting her bag. That seemed to settle him.

Mrs. Partridge was the first to spot them, her mouth falling open slightly as she did. "I just need to . . . check on some coats," she mumbled to herself before flying off fast to where they were hiding behind a billboard.

"I'm so sorry, girls," Mrs. Partridge said, her eyes close to tears. "Ernie sent the harpies to Borough Market to distract them—we had no idea *you* were headed there too."

Lina had a sudden flash of inspiration. "Wait—they think Ernie was being honest with them, but really he couldn't have known we were going there. But they don't know that?"

"No," Mrs. Partridge said with a sigh. "They think he's on their side." She looked over angrily at Miss Brown. "They're waiting for you."

"*They?*" Odge said. "All four of them?"

Mrs. Partridge shook her near-invisible head, making some of her gray curls fall loose and dangle over Lina's face. "Miss Brown is guarding the entrance; Miss Witherspoon is in the tunnel. The other two have already headed back to the mountains. They're planning a big party to celebrate the closing of the gump."

"Well, this is perfect," Odge said. "We can pick them off more easily when they're split up."

"Odge," Mrs. Partridge said, sounding aghast. "You must not attempt anything silly. You're just a young girl, and we don't need any more ghosts around here—at the rate Ernie's going, we wouldn't even have food to feed you."

Lina and the others looked over to see him devouring a floating cluster of chips. Miss Brown had her eyes fixed on him, her mouth ajar in disgusted admiration.

Mrs. Partridge spotted the King and Queen. "The royals!" she spluttered. "What . . . what are they *doing* here?"

"We collected them," Lina explained. "We couldn't leave them and have the gump close. Ben wouldn't see them for nine whole years. We're bringing them home."

"How close do you need to be to bald her?" Odge asked her aunt.

"Close," she said. "Within touching distance."

Lina took off the coat she'd been wearing since they had grabbed it from the harpies in Borough Market. "Wear this. She'll wonder how you got it, and you can get close while she questions you, and then we'll run up behind you and grab her once she's bald!"

Odge nodded, clearly impressed. "There's a problem, though. What if she recognizes you as a Gribble—she may attack. You are related to me, after all."

Lina looked over at Ernie Hobbs. "But the

harpies now trust Ernie . . . Mrs. Partridge, do you think you can get a message to him without Miss Brown hearing you?"

Aunt Maureen approached slowly, crouched, with her hands in the air. It would've been a funny sight had the humans noticed, but they were distracted by the royal couple, and many had stopped to take pictures of them, believing it to be some kind of eccentric performance piece.

It didn't take long for Miss Brown to spot Aunt Maureen.

"STOP!" she screeched.

Aunt Maureen froze on the spot.

"WHO ARE YOU?" Miss Brown demanded, squinting hard. "THAT'S OUR STOLEN COAT."

Aunt Maureen didn't say a word.

"Wait for it . . ." Odge whispered excitedly.

"I KNOW THAT FACE," Miss Brown spat. "IT'S A GRIBBLE."

"She's on our side," Ernie Hobbs said in a flat voice, as if he were reading from a piece of paper. "She hates Odge Gribble as much as the rest of us!"

"Impossible," Miss Brown said as she clawed her way closer. "Gribbles are never to be trusted. Now, which one are you?"

Lina peeked up from behind the pile of suitcases shielding her, her legs shaking.

"She's the Gribble who gave away Odge's hiding place in Borough Market," Ernie Hobbs said. "That's how I knew."

Miss Brown's expression softened, and her pursed lips rearranged themselves into a spindly grin.

"Wait for it . . ." Odge whispered again.

"Well, it seems you're the only Gribble in history to be any good," Miss Brown said with a laugh, clawing nearer.

"WAIT FOR IT . . ."

Lina leaned forward, ready to pounce.

Miss Brown inched closer and closer.

"Hang on," the harpy said, spotting Lina by the suitcases. "Is that—"

Aunt Maureen lunged forward before she could finish. An almighty cracking sound whipped around the station, causing all the humans to look up. But it hadn't come from above; it had come from the bald harpy rolling around on Platform Thirteen.

"I'M BALD!" Miss Brown screeched, stating the obvious.

Lina and Odge charged forward. The harpy tried to leap into the air, but she barely got an inch off the ground before landing back down with a squish.

Odge worked fast, tying the harpy's talons together with her bootlaces. They stood back and inspected their catch.

"YOU WON'T GET AWAY WITH THIS!" Miss Brown cried.

Lina pulled Ray out of her backpack to make room, and they stuffed Miss Brown inside. It was a fairly large backpack, and luckily harpies are surprisingly bendy.

"WHAT'S GOING ON OUT THERE?" came a cry, and through the gump shot Miss Witherspoon. She flew straight for Aunt Maureen, landing with a thud as soon as she got within touching distance.

"I'M BALD!" she screamed.

"Tie her up," Odge said, nodding at Lina's trainers.

She dutifully unthreaded them, her hands shaking as she sat on Miss Witherspoon to prevent her from scuttling away.

Soon, the pair of harpies were tied up inside the backpack. Lina spotted some chocolate éclairs lined up neatly behind Ernie Hobbs. She decided it would be nice to pop a couple in the backpack. The harpies might be hungry.

Ernie hovered over them defensively. "I'm waiting for them to go off so I can eat them," he said, reluctantly letting Lina take a few.

"Ernie Hobbs," Mrs. Partridge said sternly, "I think we both know that is not how I taught you to tidy up. You can't stash food and wait for it to go off."

"But the chocolate éclairs *never* go off," he moaned.

"Thank you for helping us," Lina said with a sad smile, knowing she might never see the ghosts again.

"You make sure you get back home safely," Mrs. Partridge said, before turning her attention to Odge. "And, Odge, you may have defeated two harpies, but don't get cocky—remember what Mrs. Smith is capable of. She will not go as easily as those two."

Odge nodded. "Spread the word to all magical creatures who were evicted from Mist that they can return," she said grandly. "There will be no harpies at the gump. They must travel home before the gump closes tonight."

"But the harpies," Mrs. Partridge said. "We can't send the magical creatures back to Mist—it would be deadly."

Odge stood tall. "Tonight, the harpies will be gone."

"But . . . it's not possible," Mrs. Partridge said.

Odge flashed Lina a smile. "Everything's possible, Mrs. Partridge. You've just been dead so long that you've forgotten."

Odge picked up the mistmaker backpack, heavy with the weight of the harpies, and slung it over her shoulder. Lina lifted Ray and wrapped him round her neck.

"We match!" Odge laughed, turning so they were standing side by side, one with a bulging mistmaker backpack on her back, the other with a real one.

Odge whistled for the King and Queen, who came running, leaving a crowd of confused humans in their wake, and together—two hags, three humans, a mistmaker, and two tied-up harpies—they made their way back to Mist for the final showdown.

CHAPTER TWENTY

THE MOUNTAIN

THE ISLAND was relatively small, but the mountain was not. It towered tall over the land, cloaked in dark clouds.

At the base of the mountain grew fields of Technicolor flowers. It had once been the home of the flower fairies and the occasional wizard, but now it lay empty, the wind combing through it as if searching for the magical creatures now scattered beyond the gumps.

It hadn't taken Lina, Odge, Aunt Maureen, and the rescued King and Queen too long to get there—the tunnel from Platform Thirteen to the shore was relatively short, and the mutant mermaids had swum them safely across the bay—but Lina noted every precious second that passed.

"We'd better keep going if we're going to make

it in time," Odge said. "The sun is setting, and I can almost feel the gumps itching to close."

"Lina, I could drop you off at that gump over there," Aunt Maureen said. "That'll take you to Tokyo. That's close to Vienna, isn't it?"

As they walked, they all repeatedly gave Lina the option to turn back. The King and Queen told Lina the story of when they'd lost Ben for nine whole years in an attempt to convince her to go home, but it was no good. She couldn't leave without seeing this through . . . to the very end.

They marched on, through the fields of flowers, but Lina soon found herself at the back—without the laces in her trainers, they kept slipping off.

"Silly things," she said, bending down to pull her left one back on.

"Speak for yourself," came a gruff voice. "And get lost—this is *our* hiding place."

Underneath a couple of large rocks, leaning together to form an arch, was a clump of flower fairies. Lina leaned down and stuck her face inside. It was rowdy in there—fairies swung each other around, smashing little tables made of bark. In the corner, a group arm-wrestled, shouting very rude words at each other when they lost.

"Lina!" Odge called back. "What are you doing?"

"Tell her and *die*," one of the flower fairies warned, brandishing his fists.

"Flower fairies," Lina said, because the last few days had made her scared of barely anyone—especially not tiny, sweet-smelling flower fairies.

It was a mistake. A stream of flower fairies flew fast at Lina's face, kicking her eyes and nose until she had to throw herself down and bury her head in the grass.

"That's quite enough," came a voice.

The flower fairies recoiled in horror at the sight of *the Queen* marching toward them. They were very badly behaved, but not in front of important and influential people. Why do you think flower fairies have such a good reputation?

"Your Majesty," they oozed, bending double, their eyes set sideways so they could glare at Lina while they did so.

"You'll come in handy," the Queen said. "We're headed up the mountain to save my son. Odge Gribble is going to stop the harpies. Come on."

"Anything, Your Majesty," they groveled.

Lina got to her feet and dusted herself off as they flew past her and joined the group. It was a long journey, but as they were about halfway up the mountain's rockiest side, Lina could make out little lights in the distance.

Thwompburg had never been a popular part of the Island—people tended to settle in the flower fields or by the cove or in the Haglands or in Central Mist, where all the action was. Ogres and trolls had built Thwompburg, and so—naturally—everything was oversized.

It had taken hours to reach the town, and Lina's feet ached. The place had character: chunky shops carved from rock sat on uneven stone streets surrounded by thundering waterfalls and tall pine trees. She climbed up onto a giant stone bench in the town square and watched as Odge ran excitedly toward a building. The hag poked her head in the door before pulling it back out and shouting, "Lina! Get over here! I want you to meet my dear friend Gurkie!"

Gurkie was a fey, and an excellent one at that. She and Odge went way back—Lina had heard—all the way back to Odge's first trip to Platform Thirteen. Gurkie, it turned out, had been kept on Mist by the harpies because they enjoyed dancing, and Gurkie was the best dance teacher on the Island. Her school was normally located in Central Mist, in a crumbling little cottage that had vegetables sprouting from the cracks. The harpies had destroyed it and relocated her to the grand old troll hospital because it was closer to their new homes.

Lina jumped down off the giant stone bench and made her way over to where Odge was standing. A sign on the door read:

GURKIE'S DANCE SCHOOL

ALL CREATURES AND VEGETABLES WELCOME!

There were harpy talon marks through the word *all*, and above it was scrawled the word *select*. They probably didn't care which vegetables attended, but Lina wondered if they'd even start policing that next.

Inside, a tall and beautiful woman with an elaborate carrot-covered hat stood poised on the very tips of her toes.

"This is her?" said the woman gently, dropping down onto her heels and gliding over to Lina. She took both Lina's hands in hers and kissed her on the cheek. "How lovely to meet you—won't you stay for my class?"

Lina could see six static beetroots lined up like dance students.

"No time to stop, Gurkie," Odge said, giving her a kiss good-bye. "We're about to bald some harpies."

"Oh, that's a shame. My beetroots aren't up to scratch this year. No dancing at all from them. I could've used some replacement dancers."

"Sorry," Lina said. "If I had been doing anything else, I would've canceled, honestly."

She stared down at the unmoving beetroots.

"Do beetroots dance sometimes?" she whispered to Odge.

"Never," Odge whispered back. "Gurkie just believes in giving vegetables the benefit of the doubt."

Gurkie picked up a stone microphone and said, "And now bend the knees!"

She looked hopefully at the beetroots.

"I thought perhaps they weren't dancing because they couldn't hear me, which is why I was using this. But now I realize it's perhaps that they don't like the microphone. Yes, that's probably it. Here, Lina—I give this microphone to you, a little reminder of our first meeting, and a present from Thwompburg."

Lina thanked her kindly as she and Odge

headed outside. Even though it was really heavy, she did rather like the microphone.

It was a blustery evening, and shop signs creaked in the wind. Odge's face fell when she saw HANS-OME CHEESES—a chunky shop with a noticeable trail of cheese stench wafting out the window.

Lina held her nose and followed Odge inside.

The place was trashed, presumably because the harpies had no desire to eat cheese.

"Ben and I used to come here for snacks," Odge said sadly. "We'd be here all day just trying to finish them."

Lina climbed up onto one of the tables and pulled open the curtains at the back of the shop. Perfectly framed by the window were the troll mansions.

"Is that them?" Lina asked. "That's where the harpies are now?"

Odge nodded. "Biggest houses on the Island. I've never been. Thwompburg is the farthest I've ever climbed up the mountain. Ben and Netty are up there somewhere. Come on—we'd better get balding if we're going to get you home in time for bed."

And so on they walked, out of the nearly deserted Thwompburg and toward the houses. The problem was, having never been there before, Odge had no idea about the drop—a deep and wide crack in the rocks separating the houses from the town. Of course, if you were a troll or an ogre, it was easy to step over, and a harpy could easily fly.

Lina stared down into the darkness. They were so close to the harpies, but they'd never make it across.

"We can carry you over," one of the flower fairies said to the King and Queen. "One at a time."

"They don't need to go over," Lina said. "It's just Aunt Maureen for the balding, and then me and Odge to tie up Miss Green and Mrs. Smith."

The flower fairy rolled her eyes. "Fine. Which one of you wants to go first?"

Lina looked up at the mansions, wondering which one was Mrs. Smith's and where Ben and Netty were being kept.

"You won't get away with this!" came the muffled shouts of Miss Brown from the mistmaker backpack.

"Aunt Maureen goes first to do the balding," Odge said. "Then me, then Lina."

The flower fairies—around a hundred of them in total—began to heave Aunt Maureen into the air. Some grabbed hold of elbows and knees, others went for the ears and the nose, and it wasn't long before she was raised up high into the air.

Lina watched in amazement, but was distracted by a whimper. She turned to see a little mistmaker hobbling toward her. It had a shorter snout than Ray and was quite a bit smaller. Behind it, two other mistmakers lay curled up and poorly. Lina ran over and stroked them.

"Do you think if I hadn't lied about being the mistmaker master the mistmakers would be better by now?" she asked Odge quietly.

"Nah," Odge said dismissively. "I don't think the mistmaker master was even going to show up, if I'm honest. She was already a minute late, and apparently the mistmaker master is never late."

"You were planning to meet the mistmaker master?" the Queen asked. "We met her just yesterday morning. She had a fabulous pigeon-feather hat."

Odge twirled round. "That's when *I* was meant to meet the mistmaker master."

Lina stood up slowly. "Pigeon-feather hat?"

"She came to the school," the King said, speaking for the first time, because he was a shy man.

"I knew Ben was worried about what was happening to the mistmakers. I thought if we summoned the mistmaker master, she could find Ben on the Island and help fix the poor creatures."

Odge threw her head back and laughed. "And of course the mistmaker master would go and meet you, because *you're* the royals. That's why she didn't meet me. Hah!"

"Did Ben not read the P.S. in our letter?" the Queen asked. "I told Miriam Hughes-Hughes to deliver it."

"We got the letter," Lina said, "but it was too deep-fat fried to read the P.S. We didn't know there was one!"

"I knew I should've used a lower setting," the Queen groaned.

"So this means you know who the mistmaker master is," Odge said excitedly. "Who is it?"

"Um, hag and human!" the flower fairies called over their shoulders. "We have a PROBLEM."

Flying fast toward them from the tallest troll house came Mrs. Smith in a vicious fury. When she saw them, she opened her mouth wide and let out the most horrifying scream Lina had ever heard. It echoed around them until they all had to drop to their knees, clutching their ears.

There was a buzz, followed by a familiar smell, and before Lina knew what was happening she was completely surrounded by swamp fairies. They tore around her, attacking at will. Lina shielded her eyes as the nasty little things bit at her face and landed on her head. She rolled about on the ground, losing hold of Ray.

"Odge!" she cried, desperately trying to see where her hag friend was.

"Over here!" Odge cried, batting away swamp fairies with a rock.

Lina looked up just in time to see the flower fairies lose their grip on Aunt Maureen. She slipped out of her jacket and let out a squeal. All Lina could do was watch as she disappeared into the deep, dark drop below.

CHAPTER TWENTY-ONE

THE HAIR ROLLERS

IT WAS the scratching noise that woke Ben. He'd fallen asleep on Netty's shoulder, and she was afraid to move. Instead, she'd sat sweating, smiling at the sound of his amateur snores.

"Did you hear that?" he said.

"Barely," Netty replied. "You really need to practice. Snoring is an art."

"Not the snoring, Netty—the scratching. See . . . there it is again!"

They both crawled slowly to the window and ducked under it.

"It sounds like something's climbing the wall. Something sharp," Ben said, his eyes wide.

Being a hag, Netty didn't spend a lot of her time being afraid of little scratching noises, so she leaped up and reached a fist out the barred window. To her surprise, her fingers touched something feathery.

She turned to Ben, a look of fear in her eyes. "I think I just grabbed Mrs. Smith."

"I'm not Mrs. Smith," came an insulted whisper. "Pull me up."

Netty did as she was told and pulled the thing through the barred window, squishing her slightly to get her through. The creature unraveled her limbs on the floor and stood up, revealing her identity. Ben gasped.

There, right in front of them, stood the horrible and hideous harpy Miss Jones.

"I thought...The other harpies said y-you went missing when the gump opened," Ben stammered, now afraid. He recognized her gaunt face from the photos of official royal events. She was the one who always floated behind his mother. Why was she here? She was as terrible as the others.

She held a thin finger to her wrinkled lips. "Your parents sent me a letter, asking me to come."

"No they didn't," Ben protested, believing it to be a trick. "They would never write to a horrible harpy."

"Bit rude," Miss Jones muttered, clearly not particularly bothered by the comment.

Netty stepped between them. "If you've come to kill Ben, then you'll have me to deal with first."

"Kill me?" Ben cried.

Miss Jones waved her arms frantically in the air. "No one here wants to kill anyone!" she shrieked.

"I do," Netty sneered, hunching over the harpy, trying to be as intimidating as possible. It didn't work, because one of the boils popped on her face and dribbled onto the floor. She stood back up, annoyed with herself.

"If you have quite finished," Miss Jones said, pushing her way past the hag and hobbling toward Ben. "I have come with news of the mistmakers."

"I don't understand," Ben whispered.

"Your parents wrote to me telling me how worried you are about the mistmakers. They asked me to help."

"But you're a harpy. I told them I needed the mistmaker master."

Miss Jones bowed. "At your service."

"You?" Ben spluttered. "You're the mysterious, marvelous mistmaker master?"

"It's a secret," Miss Jones whispered. "You know how much Mrs. Smith and the other harpies hate the mistmakers. I was the only one fascinated by the little creatures. Your parents supported me and kept it a secret. The importance of the mistmakers has always been something your parents and Mrs. Smith argued over. It's one of the things that led her to seize power—that and the fact that she hates humans. Mrs. Smith doesn't believe the mistmakers are keeping our island alive. To Mrs. Smith, the harpies are all that this island needs."

"But Odge said she searched the palace files and the address for the mistmaker master was Vienna Central Station," Ben said.

"Well, yes—that was me. When the harpy takeover happened, Mrs. Smith and all of us stormed your palace home and ransacked the place. Your parents have information about me in the palace vaults—filed under *M* for *mistmaker master*. I was terrified Mrs. Smith would find out; she'd see it as such a betrayal and against what we harpies should be standing for. So I switched the information in the file, changed the address to Vienna Central Station so the kind ghost pigeons there could deliver the letters to me. I planned to escape through the Vienna gump and head for the mountains—I wanted no part of this. Odge was very brave to go to the palace vaults for you."

"She was," Ben said with a sentimental nod. "She's always doing daring things like that for me."

"But you didn't meet Odge," Netty said to Miss Jones. "She met a human girl instead, with a weird backpack."

"Unfortunately," Miss Jones said, "I also received the letter from Ben's parents that day, asking to meet me at the exact same time. I couldn't turn down the royals. I sneakily traveled back to the Island—all the harpies were too busy rounding up magical creatures to notice me. I went through the Platform Thirteen gump and to the school to meet your parents. Afterward, I rushed back to the Island, through the Vienna hotel gump, and to the station—but Odge was gone. And so I decided to return to the Island and find you, Ben, as your parents wished. I saw Odge in the gump waiting room, but it was too dangerous to talk there."

"Well, you can talk now," Ben said eagerly. "If we can't stop Mrs. Smith, what can we do to help the mistmakers?"

"The mistmakers have always provided the mist that hides the Island. And, more than that, it protects it. You've probably noticed the strange weather? Mistmakers control so much of our island without us even knowing it. But with the harpies in charge they have given up hope—they no longer want to hide and protect the Island, because they don't believe it's worth protecting anymore. If the gump closes in a few hours, and they are trapped on this island with no hope for nine more years, they will almost certainly die"—Miss Jones bowed her head sadly—"and so will this island."

Ben looked out the window and down the mountains to what remained of his old palace home.

"If only Odge were here," he said, just as they heard Mrs. Smith scream outside.

"THEY'RE HERE! ODGE AND THE HIDEOUS LITTLE HUMAN ARE HERE!"

"FINALLY!" Netty roared, leaping up and down and banging her fists on the wall.

"What's going on in there?" came Miss Green's voice from beyond the door. She had been tasked with guarding the prisoners, which was interrupting her getting ready for the gump-closing party.

"Quick," Miss Jones said. "Hide me!"

Netty instinctively sat on her.

The door creaked open, and in strutted Miss Green. She was in a small, fluffy robe and had hair rollers in her hair, in preparation for the evening's festivities.

"What's going on in here?" she snapped.

"I think you mean, what's going on *out there*," Netty said, pointing to the window.

Miss Green flew over and stuck her head through the bars. She recoiled in shock, knocking a hair roller off.

"You dropped your—" Ben began, but Netty slapped a hand on his mouth to stop him.

"Odge and the human are back!" Miss Green seethed as she tore out of the room to the sounds of fighting below. The door locked behind her.

"We need to get down there!" Ben cried. "I think it's Lina and Odge!" He tried to squeeze his head through and look down, but it was no good. The thick walls of the tower meant only a harpy's neck was long enough to stick right out to see what was below.

Netty pulled Miss Jones out from under her— she looked furious—and picked up the hair roller and kissed it.

"Netty . . ." Ben said warily. "What are you doing?"

"Getting us out of here," she said, reaching a finger inside and pulling on a little string, like a Christmas cracker. The roller began wobbling, and she set it down quickly at the foot of the door.

And then everything went black.

There was a *click*, and the lights came back on. Ben only had a split second to take in their surroundings: the prison, the tower, the whole troll mansion had vanished!

The three of them fell fast, somersaulting through the clouds, which helped to slow them, but not enough. Miss Jones desperately clung on to them and flapped her wings. Though she wasn't strong enough to hold them up for long, it was just enough to break their fall. Ben rolled down the hill and came to a stop next to Netty.

"I booby-trapped the harpies' hair rollers with Lost Laces," Netty squealed with delight, seemingly unfazed by the near-death experience. "So that when they pulled them out of their hair, they'd pull on the laces inside and activate them—making them disappear."

"And with Lost Laces, they are invisible to you, and *you* are invisible to them," Miss Jones said. "Still, I don't see how that would've helped. Not the best plan, Netty."

"Then I was going to try to catch them somehow . . . even though they were invisible,"

Netty said. "It was more of a half-plan, really."

"And," Ben said, "by leaving the Lost Laces on the floor, rather than holding them, you made the building disappear!"

"Again," Miss Jones said, "not the best plan, Netty."

Mrs. Smith turned to the blank space where her stolen house had just been. "WHERE, CAN SOMEONE PLEASE TELL ME, IS MY MAN-SION?"

CHAPTER TWENTY-TWO
THE DROP

BACK ON the good side, Lina stared into the deep crack in the rock as Odge dropped to her knees and screamed, "AUNT MAUREEN!"

But Aunt Maureen didn't shout back.

The King and Queen ran over to comfort her.

"Why must you do this?" the Queen shouted across to Mrs. Smith, but the harpy was distracted by the invisible mansion.

"Wait a second!" a swamp fairy shouted. "I'm BALD!"

Squeaks and screams spread through the cluster of swamp and flower fairies, as each realized Aunt Maureen had blanket-balded them on the way down.

"IT TOOK ME OVER A YEAR TO GROW THAT MUSTACHE!" one of the flower fairies roared.

United in their plight, and as if they'd never had any differences to begin with, the fairies began to fly off back home to fix their hair. That's the thing about fairies—they are very fond of their hair, especially the facial hair.

"MY BEARD IS NEVER GOING TO BE THE SAME AGAIN, YOU RATBAG!" another fairy roared, waving her fist at Mrs. Smith.

At first, Mrs. Smith looked miffed—after all, the swamp fairies were her new army. But then, like this was just another exciting challenge, she whistled, and a troop of harpies emerged from the mansions behind her. Her backup army. A flock descended on Netty and Ben, completely surrounding them. Miss Jones joined them, hoping to go unnoticed.

"Where are Miss Witherspoon and Miss Brown?" Mrs. Smith snapped, but all the other harpies just shrugged. Miss Green hovered near the front, next to Mrs. Smith. As one of the most important harpies, it was only proper—even if she was in a robe and hair rollers and facing backward.

"Well," Mrs. Smith said, directing her attention toward Odge. "What are you going to do now?"

Odge furiously wiped away tears and stood up.

"I'm going to keep going until we stop you!"

"Please," Lina begged, but Mrs. Smith raised a hand to shush her.

"Sorry, human. You're too small and unimportant—I can't hear you."

Lina growled, then remembered something. She marched over to her backpack and reached inside, avoiding the harpy talons.

"Sorry," she whispered to Miss Witherspoon and Miss Brown. "I just need . . . to . . . get . . . this." She wrenched the little microphone out of the bag.

"CAN YOU HEAR ME NOW?" she shouted.

Mrs. Smith groaned and rolled her eyes. "No, you're holding it upside down."

"Oh," Lina said, flipping it round and taking a deep breath. "THIS WAS A PLACE FOR ANY-ONE WHO NEEDED IT!" her voice boomed. "WHO ARE *YOU* TO DECIDE WHO GETS TO LIVE HERE AND WHO DOESN'T?"

Mrs. Smith flew fast toward Lina and snatched something from the ground.

It took Lina a moment to realize what it was, but when she did, she turned cold.

"Ray!" she cried, racing toward the horrible harpy.

Mrs. Smith hovered, dangling Ray above the huge crack in the rocks, swaying menacingly and cackling. "I'm a harpy, you fool. Harpies once ruled this land, and now we do again! Back to the good old days! It hasn't always been filled with all these horrible humans and inferior creatures."

Lina was furious. "Who built the mountain mansions you now live in? It wasn't harpies. Who created the potions and cauldrons full of magic? It wasn't harpies. Who made this island and the magical little mistmakers who live on it? It wasn't harpies! This isn't a pair of shoes, or a handbag, or a house—it's an *island*, and it's no one's, not really. It is bigger and older than any of us. Magical creatures came to this island because it was somewhere to be safe, somewhere to belong. I can't think of a more magical island than that."

Odge gave Lina a proud nod.

Ben and Netty cheered and clapped from the other side.

"Oh, all right," Mrs. Smith said, moving closer. "Your speech changed me—you can have your little mistmaker back."

For a magical moment, Lina believed her

speech had gotten through to Mrs. Smith! She reached forward and grabbed hold of Ray's soft fur. He was shaking with fear.

"You're going to be all right," Lina said. "I promise."

In one cruel move, Mrs. Smith snatched him away, leaving Lina teetering on the edge of the drop.

"How's your balance?" the harpy hissed.

Lina stumbled, tipping forward. She frantically moved her arms like propellers, trying to will her body back, but it was no good—she tipped forward and fell into the crack.

"NO!" Odge screamed, racing to catch her, but it was too late.

Mrs. Smith flashed Odge a wicked grin.

"Oh, all right, human—you can have him," she called down, throwing Ray into the abyss after Lina.

Odge and the King and Queen stood frozen in shocked silence. Netty and Ben came running down the rocky path from the troll mansions, but stopped dead in their tracks when they realized what had just happened.

"Have we all had enough now?" Mrs. Smith said with a smirk. "Or should I continue to pick you all off like old boils?"

CHAPTER TWENTY-THREE

THE AUNTS

THE FALL seemed to go on forever, but it did end—and, when it did, it wasn't what Lina expected at all.

She landed with a thud on an ogre-sized wooden table wedged between the rocks. It was dark down there, with only the odd dull streaks of exhausted light able to reach through. The table groaned under her weight.

"Isn't it funny," came a familiar voice from the darkness, "to be stuck in this drop atop a pile of giant furniture? This is not how I thought my day would go when I woke up this morning!"

"Aunt Maureen!" Lina cried, leaning over to see the hag settled on a large footstool below her, and in her arms Lina was thrilled to see Ray.

"They've obviously been renovating the troll

mansions," Aunt Maureen said. "I did hear they were getting the hags to throw everything out—they must've thrown it all down here."

Lina looked up to the thin strip of light above. The problem was now how to get back up, or else they would be stuck here, stranded forever.

"How's it going up there?" Aunt Maureen asked hopefully. "Good?"

A cluster of ghosts materialized in front of Lina.

"Oh dear, look at her," one said, pulling a frown.

"So sad and helpless!" another said.

"This is quite the pickle," said the third.

"You look stuck," the fourth one said.

"Who . . . who are you?" Lina whispered.

"We're the aunts," they said in unison. "And if you're stuck then we're here to help."

"Oh good," Lina said, collapsing on the table. "You could lift me up and Aunt Maureen down there too."

"No can do," said the first one. "You're too heavy."

"We're old aunts," the fourth one said.

"But, please, I need your help," Lina begged. "I'm stuck like the furniture."

They all smiled. "Just look around. It's not just

troll furniture that's been left down here." And with that they were gone!

Lina shakily got to her feet, and the table groaned again.

"Careful," Aunt Maureen said. "We don't want you falling farther."

"We need to get back up. There *must* be a way."

"Sometimes, there isn't a way," Aunt Maureen said. "That's just the way of it."

Lina spotted something. It was small, and had she not been desperately hoping for something like it she may never have noticed it. But there it was, shimmering slightly in the light—a small, perfectly round stone. She waved her hand close to it.

"What are you doing up there?" Aunt Maureen asked, shifting on the stool to get a better look.

Lina grinned and pushed the stone, cracking the surface of it. She watched in amazement as a glistening liquid dribbled out of it and down into the depths below.

"Cor's enchantments," Lina whispered with a smile. "I hope this one is more useful than the mood cloud Odge found."

"What was that?" Aunt Maureen said, squinting to see. "Sounded like a boil being popped."

There was a rumble. The furniture began to shake.

"COR BLIMEY!" Lina cried as out of the depths burst the most magnificent bagworm, its body bigger than a train carriage and its skin more gilded than a palace ballroom. It slithered up and around them, scooping them up.

"Fairies' nostril hair, will you look at that!" Aunt Maureen cried, grabbing hold of Ray.

"Odge and Ben told me that a wizard called Cor had left his magic scattered across the Island," Lina said. "And am I glad he did!"

Aunt Maureen nodded approvingly. "Well, well—a bagworm from Cor. What are we waiting for? Let's go and get them."

Bagworms are incredibly rare, and very few magical creatures on Mist have ever seen one. So it made for an excellent entrance.

The bagworm shot out of the deep hole between the rocks, startling Mrs. Smith. She tumbled backward, close enough for Aunt Maureen to bald her instantly. The other harpies fell to the ground with a thud too, their featherless bodies rolling around.

Lina steered the bagworm and let it flop

down, creating a bridge for the others to cross. They flooded over to the other side—Odge, the King, the Queen, even Gurkie, who had heard the commotion and shown up with her motionless beetroots, in case they might be of use. They joined Ben and Netty and quickly gathered the harpies.

Mrs. Smith clawed her way across the ground, grabbing fistfuls of dirt and throwing them at anyone who came close. Lina and Odge followed slowly behind her.

"YOU CAN'T DEFEAT ME!" she roared. "I'M UNSTOPPABLE! IT'S IMPOSSIBLE!"

Odge kneeled down next to Mrs. Smith. "Nothing's impossible, I'm afraid."

Mrs. Smith tried to grab her with a talon, but Odge was too quick.

"I *knew* you were planning something with that human-looking girl!" Mrs. Smith growled. "What is she really? A witch? A demon? A WHAT?"

"She's just a human," Odge said with a smile.

Lina nodded proudly. "With a very handy backpack."

"Take them away," the Queen commanded as Gurkie gently tied up Mrs. Smith, placing a beetroot on her head for good vibes.

The King rushed over to Ben, scooping him into his arms.

Netty punched the air in victory. "MIST IS BACK!" Her eyelashes flashed orange, and streaks of lightning split the sky.

Odge hugged Lina tightly, then flopped onto the ground, completely exhausted.

And for the first time in nine long days, Mist was peaceful.

"THE TIME!" Odge roared. "I completely forgot! We need to get Lina to the gump!"

CHAPTER TWENTY-FOUR

THE TIME!

NETTY BIT her boily lip. "I don't think we can make it . . . The Vienna gump is way down by Central Mist."

Lina stared down the mountain. The moon was rising in the sky, and mist from the happy mistmakers curled up and around the trees as if reclaiming the Island once more. She looked past Thwompburg and the flower fields and traced her finger down the half-moon-shaped cove to the town square. Under it lay the tunnels—the tunnel to her gump.

There was a cough.

Lina spun round to see Miss Jones the harpy standing there.

"If you don't mind, I'd like to volunteer myself to help, and so would my reformed friend, Miss Green."

Miss Green walked backward toward them and nodded.

"If your aunt could unbald us, Odge, we could fly the girl to the gump. We're the strongest—and the fastest. I don't mean to brag. That's just a fact."

Odge and the others exchanged skeptical glances.

"She has always been on our side," Ben interjected. "Miss Jones can be trusted."

Lina smiled. "I trust them."

"You can trust us too!" came a muffled shout from inside Lina's backpack.

"Oh dear!" Lina said. "I forgot about you two." She unzipped the backpack and freed Miss Witherspoon and Miss Brown.

Odge gave the nod, and Aunt Maureen unbalded them. They flew up into the air and circled round Lina's head.

"Your backpack," Odge said, looping it over Lina's shoulders. "Take care of it."

Lina threw herself into Odge's arms. "I don't want to go. I'll miss you all too much."

"You must," Odge said sadly. "But we'll meet again one day—I just know it."

"But I feel so at home here on Mist. What if I don't feel at home in Vienna anymore?" Lina said.

Odge hugged her tightly. "Lina, you can belong to more than one place. You don't have to choose. Mist can be where your heart is, and another part of it can be in Vienna." She gave another nod, and the harpies grabbed hold of Lina's backpack straps, lifting her high into the air.

Everyone gathered and waved as Lina sailed off down the mountain. She looked back and saw Odge and Ben running fast after her, smiling and laughing and trying to catch up.

"WE LOVE YOU, LINA!" they cried.

She wanted to shout something, something to show how much she cared. But every word got caught in her throat as she choked back tears. All she could do was wave.

All across the Island, magical creatures spilled from gumps, happy to be home once again.

Ben and Odge stopped when they reached the flower field and doubled over, out of breath. Lina waved as she watched them get smaller and smaller, her favorite hag and the human prince standing in a field, arm in arm in the moonlight.

She had to run through the tunnel on her own because the harpies couldn't fly down there.

She could see the swirling portal slowly closing.

And then she saw Hans, his cheese-colored beard, dipping in and out of the gump.

"Hans!" she cried. "Come on! The gump is about to close! We stopped the harpies. Quick!"

Hans shook his head and reached out a hand to help her through.

"I stay in Vienna." He dropped a Vienna post-card onto the floor.

Lina picked it up. It simply said:

Odge,

    I decide to stay with my parents.
    They need me.
    See you soon.
    LOOK AFTER HANS-OME CHEESES

Lina took his hand, and he pulled her through, with only a second to spare.

"No!" she said, as the gump fizzed and vanished. "I forgot to say good-bye to Ray!"

Lina stared at the hotel bathroom where the gump had just been. It was as if it had never been there at all.

Magdelena appeared with a *pop*. "Oh good! You're right on time. Now, I must warn you, Miriam Hughes-Hughes visited your parents and told them everything. They have arrived to collect you. I'm glad you made it—I was steeling myself to break it to your parents that they might not see you for nine years. I can't imagine that's very comforting news to hear from a ghost rat."

Lina walked sadly toward the lifts, but Hans, having spotted what was in her backpack, couldn't stop smiling.

"What are you smiling at, Hans?" Lina asked.

"ODGE GAVE LINA VERY GOOD BIRTH-DAY PRESENT."

CHAPTER TWENTY-FIVE

THE END

LINA LASKY was bursting to tell her parents everything.

"I know Miriam Hughes-Hughes has updated you, but it gets even better," Lina said to her parents as she climbed into bed.

"You should sleep now," her father said. "In the morning, we'll talk about everyth—"

"I've been on Mist, saving the Island from some terrible harpies! I met a famous hag, and she became my friend. I ate a chocolate bar that a maggot vomited up. I disguised myself as a rock monster, went to London, and met the world's best balder and the pearly mermaids, who showed me their sewer. I saw beetroots dancing and fell to what I thought was my death, but an unwanted troll table saved me. I told off an evil harpy and saved an island. I had the most magical birthday.

I'm really, truly sorry if I worried you. Next time I do something like that, I'll tell you first."

"Oh, Lina! We're just glad you're home," her mother said.

Miriam Hughes-Hughes popped her head through the door. "We've been having a great time! They fainted initially on seeing me, but we've had some wonderful conversations since."

"We . . . we now know that magic is real," her father said, sounding more than a little bewildered. "And we have confirmed with our new ghost friend that your aunt's neighbor Mrs. Frampton is, in fact, a witch. So . . . that's nice."

"I've been educating them," Miriam Hughes-Hughes said with a wink.

"Oh," Lina added. "And I opened my backpack when I got home and found my new friends had put Ray in there. Ray is a mistmaker, and, as they said in their note, he's old and in need of a retirement home. We bonded on Mist, and he'll be living under my bed enjoying old age, and I might occasionally take him for walks in my backpack. Anyway, that's all, and that's the truth," she finished.

Her parents said goodnight and slowly retreated, exchanging fast whispers.

Once they were gone, Lina pulled a newspaper

article out from under her pillow and smiled at the picture that accompanied it. It showed her standing next to Hans, who was towering over his two not-at-all-ogre-like parents. They looked overcome with joy to be with him again. She scooped Ray up from under the bed, letting him snuggle into the pillow.

A MAGIC FEAST

Vienna is abuzz this evening with the news that the little girl who disappeared from Vienna Central Station was found under a table in the Sacher Hotel, where she had been eating torte. None of the staff had noticed her.

Lina Lasky was found by a very kind and substantial local gentleman called Hans. He had been dining there with his elderly parents, with whom he was recently reunited after a long stint making cheese abroad.

The hotel says Lina is welcome back anytime.

Lina carefully folded the newspaper and tucked it under her pillow.

"Goodnight, Odge," she whispered.

It would be nine long years before they would

meet again, but what wonderful memories she had to keep her company until that day came. Lina pulled the duvet up under her chin and smiled. And somewhere, way out there beyond the gump, Odge did the same.

ACKNOWLEDGMENTS

I first read *The Secret of Platform 13* when I was nine years old, and I fell in love with Eva Ibbotson's world. To be allowed behind the scenes has been beyond magical for this grown-up superfan. Thank you to the wonderful Ibbotson family for trusting me with this project, and special thanks to Justin Ibbotson for his kind, confidence-boosting words, for inviting me to stop by for tea anytime, and for making me feel so welcome in his mother's world. Eva made magical books and even more magical people, and it has been such an honor to live in her worlds—both real and imagined—if only for a while. Thank you, I will never forget it.

Thank you to the marvelous Lucy Pearse—it has been such a fun journey working on this book with someone so talented and passionate about honeymoon in Vienna into a research trip, and thank you to my family, especially my mum and dad, who kept my original copy of *The Secret of Platform 13* all these years.

Thank you to my wonderful writer friends, especially Team Cooper, and my lovely non-writer friends—special thanks to Tommy Seddon, for being my unofficial publicist from the very beginning. And thank you to my incomparable readers, the craziest kids in the country, who never fail to inspire me.

Thank you to my favorite Frankie Cordall, who inspired the truly kind, courageous, and magical new characters in this book.

And thank you, Eva—you filled my childhood with so much magic, and continue to do so for so many others. We are so lucky we get to keep your magic forever.

ABOUT THE AUTHORS

SIBÉAL POUNDER is the author of the bestselling Witch Wars and Bad Mermaids series, as well as the World Book Day mash-up *Bad Mermaids Meet the Witches*. Before becoming a full-time author, Sibéal worked as a writer and researcher for the *Financial Times*, with other writing credits including *Vogue* and *Glamour* online magazines. *Beyond Platform 13*, the sequel to Eva Ibbotson's classic *The Secret of Platform 13*, is Sibéal's first stand-alone novel.

EVA IBBOTSON was born in Vienna, but when the Nazis came to power, her family fled to England and she was sent to boarding school. She became a writer while bringing up her four children, and her bestselling novels have been published around the world. *Journey to the River Sea* won the Nestlé Gold Award and was short-listed for the Carnegie Medal, the Whitbread Children's Book of the Year, and the *Guardian* Children's Fiction Prize. Some of her other young fiction titles include *The Great Ghost Rescue*, *Which Witch?*, and *Dial a Ghost*. Eva died peacefully in October 2010 at the age of eighty-five.

Turn the page to read the first chapter of
Eva Ibbotson's beloved classic
The Secret of Platform 13!

ONE

IF YOU went into a school nowadays and said to the children: "What is a *gump*?" you would probably get some very silly answers.

"It's a person without a brain, like a chump," a child might say. Or:

"It's a camel whose hump has got stuck." Or even:

"It's a kind of chewing gum."

But once this wasn't so. Once every child in the land could have told you that a gump was a special mound, a grassy bump on the earth, and that in this bump was a hidden door which opened every so often to reveal a tunnel which led to a completely different world.

They would have known that every country has its own gump and that in Great Britain the gump was in a place called the Hill of the Cross of Kings not far from the River Thames. And the wise children, the ones that read the old stories and listened to the old tales, would have known more than that. They would have known that this particular gump opened for exactly nine days every nine years, and not one second longer, and that it was no good changing your mind about coming or going because nothing would open the door once the time was up.

But the children forgot—everyone forgot— and perhaps you can't blame them, yet the gump is still there. It is under Platform Thirteen of King's Cross Railway Station, and the secret door is behind the wall of the old gentlemen's cloakroom with its flappy posters saying "Trains Get You There" and its chipped wooden benches and the dirty ashtrays in which the old gentlemen used to stub out their smelly cigarettes.

No one uses the platform now. They have built newer, smarter platforms with rows of shiny luggage trolleys and slot machines that actually work and television screens which show you how late your train is going to be. But Platform Thirteen is different. The clock has stopped; spiders have spun their webs across the cloakroom door. There's a Left-Luggage Office with a notice saying NOT IN USE, and inside it is an umbrella covered in mold which a lady left on the 5:25 from Doncaster the year of the Queen's Silver Jubilee. The chocolate machines are rusty and lopsided, and if you were foolish enough to put your money in one it would make a noise like "Harrumph" and swallow it, and you could wait the rest of your life for the chocolate to come out.

Yet when people tried to pull down that part of the station and redevelop it, something always went wrong. An architect who wanted to build shops there suddenly came out in awful boils and went to live in Spain, and when they tried to re-lay the tracks for electricity, the surveyor said the ground wasn't suitable and muttered *something* about subsidence and cracks. It was as though people knew *something* about Platform Thirteen, but they didn't know what.

But in every city there are those who have not forgotten the old days or the old stories. The ghosts, for example . . . Ernie Hobbs, the railway porter who'd spent all his life working at King's Cross and still liked to haunt round the trains, he knew—and so did his friend, the ghost of a cleaning lady called Mrs. Partridge who used to scrub out the parcels' office on her hands and knees. The people who plodged about in the sewers under the city and came up occasionally through the manholes beside the station, they knew . . . and so in their own way did the pigeons.

They knew that the gump was still there and they knew where it led. By a long, misty, and mysterious tunnel to a secret cove where a ship waited to take those who wished it to an island so beautiful that it took the breath away.

The people who lived on it just called it the Island, but it has had all sorts of names: Avalon, St. Martin's Land, the Place of the Sudden Mists. Years and years ago it was joined to the mainland, but then it broke off and floated away slowly westward, just as Madagascar floated away from the continent of Africa. Islands do that every few million years; it is nothing to make a fuss about.

With the floating island, of course, came the people who were living on it: sensible people mostly who understood that everyone did not have to have exactly two arms and legs, but might be different in shape and different in the way they thought. So they lived peacefully with ogres who had one eye or dragons (of whom there were a lot about in those days). They didn't leap into the sea every time they saw a mermaid comb her hair on a rock. They simply said, "Good morning." They understood that Ellerwomen had hollow backs and hated to be looked at on a Saturday and that if trolls wanted to wear their beards so long that they stepped on them every time they walked, then that was entirely their own affair.

They lived in peace with the animals too. There were a lot of interesting animals on the Island as well as ordinary sheep and cows and goats. Giant birds who had forgotten how to fly and laid eggs the size of kettle drums, and brollachans like blobs of jelly with dark red eyes, and sea horses with manes of silk which galloped and snorted in the waves.

But it was the mistmakers that the people of the Island loved the most. These endearing animals are found nowhere else in the world. They are white and small with soft fur all over their bodies, rather like baby seals, but they don't have flippers. They have short legs and big feet like the feet of puppies. Their black eyes are huge and moist, their noses are whiskery and cool, and they pant a little as they move because they look rather like small pillows and they don't like going very fast.

The mistmakers weren't just *nice*, they were exceedingly important.

Because as the years passed and newspapers were washed up on the shore or refugees came through the gump with stories of the World Above, the Islanders became more and more determined to be left alone. Of course they knew that some modern inventions were good, like electric blankets to keep people's feet warm in bed or fluoride to stop their teeth from rotting, but there were other things they didn't like at all, like nuclear weapons or tower blocks at the tops of which old ladies shivered and shook because the lifts were bust, or battery hens stuffed two in a cage. And they dreaded being discovered by passing ships or airplanes flying too low.

Which is where the mistmakers came in. These sensitive creatures, you see, absolutely adore music. When you play music to a mistmaker, its eyes grow wide and it lets out its breath and gives a great sigh.

"Aaah," it will sigh. "Aaah . . . aaah . . ."

And each time it sighs, mist comes from its mouth: clean, thick, white mist which smells of early morning and damp grass. There are hundreds and hundreds of mistmakers lolloping over the turf or along the shore of the Island, and that means a lot of mist.

So when a ship was sighted or a speck in the sky which might be an airplane, all the children ran out of school with their flutes and their trumpets and their recorders and started to play to the mistmakers . . . And the people who might have landed and poked and pried saw only clouds of whiteness and went on their way.

Though there were so many unusual creatures on the Island, the royal family was entirely human and always had been. They were royal in the proper sense—not greedy, not covered in jewels, but brave and fair. They saw themselves as servants of the people, which is how all good rulers should think of themselves, but often don't.

The King and Queen didn't live in a golden palace full of uncomfortable gilded thrones which stuck into people's behinds when they sat down, nor did they fill the place with servants who fell over footstools from walking backward from Their Majesties. They lived in a low white house on a curving beach of golden sand studded with cowrie shells—and always, day or night, they could hear the murmur and slap of the waves and the gentle soughing of the wind.

The rooms of the palace were simple and cool;

the windows were kept open so that birds could fly in and out. Intelligent dogs lay sleeping by the hearth; bowls of fresh fruit and fragrant flowers stood on the tables. And anyone who had nowhere to go—orphaned little hags or seals with sore flippers or wizards who had become depressed and old—found sanctuary there.

And in the year 1983—the year the Americans put a woman into space—the Queen, who was young and kind and beautiful, had a baby. Which is where this story really begins.

The baby was a boy, and it was everything a baby should be, with bright eyes, a funny tuft of hair, a button nose, and interesting ears. Not only that, but the little Prince could whistle before he was a month old—not proper tunes, but a nice peeping noise like a young bird.

The Queen was absolutely besotted about her son, and the King was so happy that he thought he would burst, and all over the Island the people rejoiced because you can tell very early how a baby is going to turn out, and they could see that the Prince was going to be just the kind of ruler that they wanted.

Of course as soon as the child was born, there

were queues of people round the palace wanting to look after him and be his nurse: Wise Women who wanted to teach him things and sirens who wanted to sing to him and hags who wanted to show him weird tricks. There was even a mermaid who seemed to think she could look after a baby, even if it meant she had to be trundled round the palace in a bath on wheels.

But although the Queen thanked everyone most politely, the nurse she chose for her baby was an ordinary human. Or rather it was three ordinary humans: triplets whose names were Violet and Lily and Rose. They had come to the Island as young girls and were proper trained nursery nurses who knew how to change nappies and bring up wind and sieve vegetables, and the fact that they couldn't do any magic was a relief to the Queen, who sometimes felt she had enough magic in her life. Having triplets seemed to her a good idea because looking after babies goes on night and day and this way there would always be someone with spiky red hair and a long nose and freckles to soothe the Prince and rock him and sing to him, and he wouldn't be startled by the change because however remarkable the baby was, he wouldn't be able to tell Violet from Lily or Lily from Rose.

So the three nurses came and they did indeed look after the Prince most devotedly and everything went beautifully—for a while. But when the baby was three months old, there came the time of the Opening of the Gump—and after that, nothing was ever the same again.